RARY

SEVENTH GRADE vs. THE GALAXY

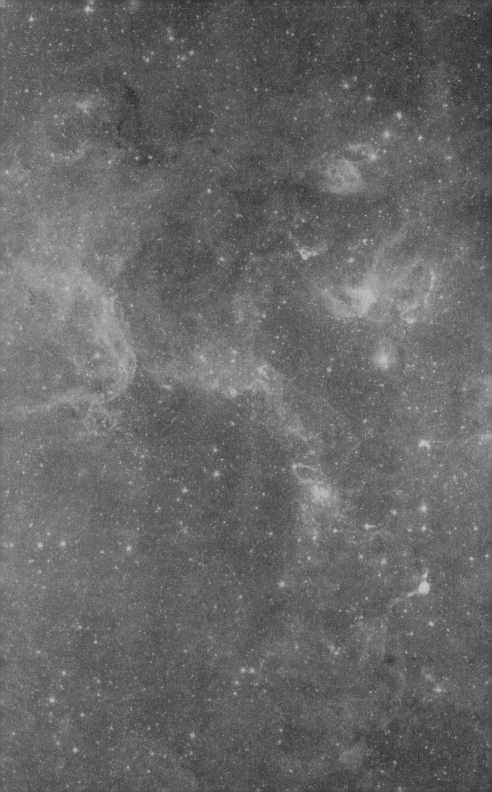

SEVENTH GRADE VS. THE GALAXY

JOSHUA S. LEVY

CAROLRHODA BOOKS
MINNEAPOLIS

Carolrhoda Books
A division of Lerner Publishing Group, Inc.
241 First Avenue North
Minneapolis, MN 55401 USA

For reading levels and more information, look up this title at www.lernerbooks.com.

Cover illustration by Petur Antonsson.
Design elements by Triff/Shutterstock.com (galaxy); mapichai/Shutterstock.com (rays).
Map © Laura Westlund/Independent Picture Service.

Main body text set in Bembo Std regular 12.5/17.
Typeface provided by Monotype Typography.

Library of Congress Cataloging-in-Publication Data

Names: Levy, Joshua (Joshua S.), author.
Title: Seventh grade vs. the galaxy / by Joshua Levy.
Other titles: Seventh grade versus the galaxy
Description: Minneapolis, MN : Carolrhoda Books, Lerner Publishing Group, [2019] |
    Summary: In 2299, seventh-grader Jack and his classmates find themselves in hostile
    alien territory after Jack accidentally launches their rickety public schoolship light
    years away from home.
Identifiers: LCCN 2018010973 (print) | LCCN 2018017705 (ebook) |
    ISBN 9781541541818 (eb pdf) | ISBN 9781541528109 (th : alk. paper)
Subjects: | CYAC: Adventure and adventurers—Fiction. | Space ships—Fiction. |
    Schools—Fiction. | Life on other planets—Fiction. | Science fiction. | Humorous
    stories.
Classification: LCC PZ7.1.L4895 (ebook) | LCC PZ7.1.L4895 Sev 2019 (print) | DDC
    [Fic]—dc23

LC record available at https://lccn.loc.gov/2018010973

Manufactured in the United States of America
1-44686-35525-10/19/2018

Tali & Serena: More than anyone,
I'd take this road with you. Also, this
doesn't count as going into space.

P.S.S. 118—Main Level Fire-Escape Plan

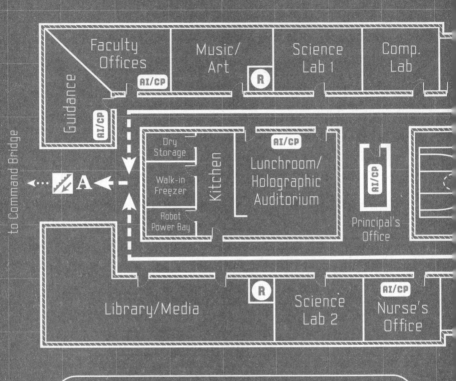

to Command Bridge

Faculty Offices

Guidance

AI/CP

AI/CP

Music/ Art

R

Science Lab 1

Comp. Lab

Dry Storage

Walk-in Freezer

Robot Power Bay

Kitchen

AI/CP

Lunchroom/ Holographic Auditorium

AI/CP

Principal's Office

A

Library/Media

R

Science Lab 2

AI/CP

Nurse's Office

A Stairwell to: engineering; reclamation; fuel/water/oxygen stores

B Stairwell to: hangar bay/exit; flight & maintenance crew quarters; faculty quarters

C Stairwell to: hangar bay/exit; gravitometric field generator; teachers' lounge

AI/CP A.I. Interface/Control Access Panel

→ Primary Exit Route

◄-- Secondary Exit Route

◇ Restricted Access Hatch

R Restroom and shower

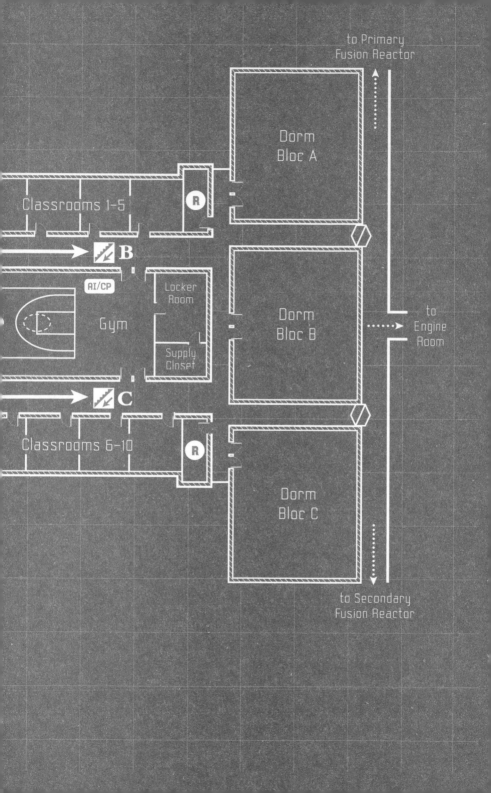

1

Zero-gravity dodgeball three times since Tuesday. So you *know* it's the end of the year.

I shuffle toward the back wall of the gym and line up behind the rest of the class. If I ever get picked first for dodgeball, it'll mean the universe has turned upside down.

"Becka!" shouts Riya Windsor, one of the team captains.

Becka Pierce trots over to the other side of the gym and gives Riya a high five that sounds like a sonic boom. I watch Riya wince and pretend that she doesn't feel like she just slapped a brick wall.

"Shocker," I whisper to Ari. Becka's always first pick—not that this bothers me, but I'm hoping I at least don't get picked *last* today. This has officially been the worst year of my life. And I'd like to get through the next few hours without being reminded *again* that I'm the least popular kid onboard the PSS 118.

Ari doesn't say a word, probably because he can't hear me over the thumps in his chest. He's had this cartoon crush on Becka for as long as I can remember. The kind where your heart pops out against your shirt, you go all bug-eyed for no reason, and little pink hearts float up out of your head like bubbles.

It's super annoying.

I don't know why he likes her so much. She kind of scares me. And during gym class, she's a freaking nightmare. Literally. Once, after a really intense game of freeze tag, my dorm-mate Diego woke up in the middle of the night, covered in sweat, screaming, "No, Becka! I'm *not* it! Please! I'm *not* it!"

"T-Bex! T-Bex!" some of our classmates cheer.

Becka flashes one of her evil grins. She's tall, maybe the tallest girl in the whole school. And a couple of years ago, Hunter LaFleur started calling her "Tyrannosaurus Bex," or "T-Bex" for short. So naturally, she showed up to the school dance in a giant dinosaur costume (who knows where she even got that from) and shoved Hunter into the drink table. He slipped on some spilled fruit punch and broke one of his big toes when he tried to get up. They didn't even *have* detention in fifth grade before that day. But Becka didn't care about getting in trouble. She beamed all the way to Principal Lochner's office. And now "T-Bex" isn't an insult. It's a term of respect.

"Can't believe we're playing dodgeball again," I tell him.

"What?" Ari says, hypnotized by the *snap snap* beat of Becka cracking her knuckles.

Ordinarily, I would slap him on the back of the head to bring him to his senses, but I resist the urge. Things have been bad enough between us lately. (Long story. My fault.) I don't want to strain our friendship even more. Especially because he's the only person who didn't start treating me differently after my dad—aka our science teacher—got fired a few months ago.

So I just mutter, "Creeper alert."

Which Ari understands right away. "Oh." He tears his eyes away from Becka. "Thanks."

"Anyway, I was saying that I can't believe we're playing this again." I know we're still on the same page about most things, including disliking dodgeball. Of course, Ari holds the high score in *Virtual* Dodgeball (along with every other video game I know). But the real thing? Not so much.

"Eh," he responds, pointing to the corner of the room. Ms. Needle—who teaches mismatched things like PE, music, art, and Spanish (and dresses like she's getting ready for all those classes at once)—is lost in some old-timey paper book that she must've checked out from the special library on Ceres. "There's nothing else she can get us to play on the last day of school without having to yell."

I nod. Can't blame Ms. Needle for being a little

burned out. I'd be, too, if I was an underpaid public school teacher who spent nine months of the year living with my whiny students onboard a rundown spaceship. My dad used to say that it's "the most rewarding job in the solar system." But my dad's also a liar.

"And second," Ari adds, "dodgeball isn't my favorite either. But don't jinx yourself by complaining. It's bad luck. The ball will for sure knock out your teeth or something."

That's Ari: something practical and smart, because he's brilliant, immediately followed by something ridiculous and superstitious, because—and I've never been totally clear on this—maybe he also believes in magic? But he's right about one thing: I don't need any more bad luck.

"Come on!" Hunter shouts at the captains. "We're not gonna have enough time!"

"Okay, okay," Riya groans, rubbing her forehead. She's clearly having trouble picking between the only two choices left. Unlike Becka, Ari and I are short and scrawny. Ari has giant dark hair that always looks like he just finished electrocuting himself. (And considering his habit of tinkering with every machine he can get his hands on, he sometimes really has just finished electrocuting himself.) I have super freckly skin and eyes that I've always thought are a little too big for my face. You'd know just by looking at us that we aren't the next All-Jupiter Athletes in the making.

"Fine," Riya says, throwing up her hands. "I guess I pick Ari."

I sigh. The other captain doesn't bother to call my name, even for the ceremony of it. He just glares at me and shrugs.

***

Thwack. Becka is in one of her frenzies. It's not easy to throw in zero gravity, but Becka manages just fine. She hurls the ball at Gena Korematsu so hard that it actually hits Gena's stomach and bounces directly back into Becka's hands so she can have another go. Gena flies over to the sidelines, spinning out of control. Becka kicks off the wall and rockets across the room. Halfway to the other side, she fakes the ball at Hunter's head. And Hunter—twenty feet up in the air—curls up like a scared hedgehog. But as Becka crosses directly in front of Hunter, she just taunts him with a wave and a smile. People would probably be more upset about Becka hogging the ball if we weren't all so busy keeping away from her.

Like the rest of our school, the gym is nothing special. Correction: It's *un*special. Subspecial. It's about the size of a basketball court, with crooked baskets attached to the roof at each end and bleachers on one side that used to fold down onto the floor but have been stuck half-open for two years. Principal Lochner likes to joke that "the money to fix the bleachers should come in *any day* now!" Because, like most of the other public schoolships orbiting Jupiter's moons, we're basically broke. Check out the PE supply closet: busted hockey sticks, useless tug-of-war bungee straps, torn jump ropes tied together, and a stack of orange cones that look like they've been blasted through the thickest part of the Kuiper belt. This dodgeball is our *last* ball—we use it for dodgeball, kickball, volleyball, basketball, and a very frustrating version of touch football.

Trying to avoid getting hit, Cal Brown instead gets caught up in one of the "GO CHAMPIONS!" banners that dangles from the ceiling. Everyone laughs, and not only because Cal is a klutz. Since none of our teams has ever won even a single championship for *any* sport—even with Becka leading the pack—the school's nickname has turned into a bitter inside joke.

Becka spits into her hands and rubs them together to improve her grip, which is an even grosser thing to do in zero-g than normal. Ari stops to stare at her like she's a glowing angel dancing in slow motion.

Thwack. Thwack. Thwack.

Becka does her signature move: she smacks the ball into a steady spin and holds a finger an inch or two underneath it like she's levitating it with her mind. More than a little distracted today, I fail to immediately notice that I'm the only one left on my team.

"You ready for the pain, Graham?" Becka asks.

The class is buzzing: Jack Graham is no match for a roaring T-Bex hunting its prey. Fine by me. There's plenty of time for a second game, which I plan to actually pay attention to—just enough to get out toward the beginning and spend the rest of the period hovering alone in the corner.

But as the ball shoots toward me like a laser bolt, some uncontrollable instinct takes over and I flail my arms up to block it. To be fair, I'm pretty sure that, had it hit my stomach, it would have done permanent damage to my kidneys. So I make a fist. Strike the ball. And smack it down toward the bleachers, where it hits the edge of one of the long benches and somehow—

Bang.

—the ball pops, leaving behind a sad rubber pancake floating in the air.

Ari was right. I shouldn't have jinxed it.

Just like our ball—our very last ball—the room explodes.

"Come on!"

"You had to try, didn't you?"

"Worst. Game. Ever."

"You should have gone home with your dad!"

At that last comment, the gym goes silent and I flinch worse than when the dodgeball was barreling toward me. It would have been less painful if I'd let it crush my internal organs. I shut my eyes tight and try to push down the urge to flee the gym, run to my dorm, and never come out. I just wanted to get through one day without having to hear someone mention my dad.

I haven't seen him in months and part of me doesn't want to see him ever again. Of course, it's the last day of school. So this afternoon I'll be on a shuttle heading down to Ganymede, and I'll have to spend the whole summer with him. I would've preferred a few hours of peace, a few hours of flying under the radar, before having to deal with all that.

Sure, it's always been a little weird to be a teacher's kid. But I was never an outcast before. And my dad wasn't just a science teacher—he's a legit scientist with a PhD from the University of California–Europa. The other kids actually thought he was *cool*, which made me cool by extension. He could've kept his cushy job at NASA, but he decided to teach middle-school science on a public schoolship instead because he "believed in the importance of public education" and was "passionate about teaching the next generation" and "wanted to spend more time with his son" and—lots of other things I'd also put in quotes because I don't believe them anymore.

And sure, life wasn't perfect. Especially after my parents got divorced and my mom moved all the way to Earth. But I was reasonably popular. I was smart. (Okay, fine, but I used to get B's, do you hear me? *B's!*) And I was happy. But then my dear old dad went and got himself fired right after winter break, and things got bad. Like—"Jack, these nice people from the Department of Homeland Security have a few questions for you about your father"—bad.

And that was only the beginning of my problems.

"Ms. Needle!" someone shouts. "Ms. Needle!"

Floating around by the emergency exit sign, she looks up from her book at what's left of the ball, sees everyone staring at me, and sighs.

"Well, accidents happen," she says too sweetly, like she's talking to a dying puppy. I'm afraid she might fly over to me and scratch behind my ears.

It's in her voice and in her eyes. *Poor little Jack Graham has been through enough already.* She was friends with my dad before he was kicked off the ship and still hasn't said a bad word about him. But I don't know who makes me feel worse, the kids who hate me or the adults who feel sorry for me.

She pulls herself over to the nearest control panel, presses an open hand against the scanner, and lets it read her palm and fingerprints.

"*WELCOME, ARGENTINA NEEDLE,*" the computer says in its whiny, nasally voice. "*KIDS GET TIRED ALREADY?*"

As AIs go, ours can be a little sarcastic.

"No!" the class groans.

"It's time to go anyway," Ms. Needle says, even though it's not. "Ship, reengage the gym's gravity."

"*GOT IT*," says the ship. "*TEACHER GOT TIRED ALREADY.*"

And we all start floating back down to the floor, even though there are fifteen whole minutes left to the period. I look into a few faces and know exactly what they're thinking: "One more thing ruined by the Graham family."

Could this day get any worse?

2

Principal Lochner steps over to his podium. He's wearing the wrinkled suit he always wears, with a half-tucked-in, button-down shirt and a tie with rubber duckies on it. I've been going to this school for three years and I don't think I've ever seen his jacket close all the way. Any second now, the shirt buttons straining against his belly are going to pop off and poke some fifth graders' eyes out. So basically, he's perfect for the PSS 118.

"What a year!" he begins.

No kidding.

We're in the cafeteria for the end-of-the-year assembly. The tables and benches have been folded and stacked in a corner, replaced by rows of rusty metal folding chairs. Next door in the kitchen, I can see the three old lunch robots—nicknamed Cranky, Creaky, and Stingy—slumped over today's leftovers of mac and cheese and potato wedges. The robots hate assemblies even more than we do, so they turn themselves off as soon as the principal starts speaking. One of the teachers will have to power them up again manually afterward. Once, Cranky was offline for a week after it hid behind the fridge for its nap and no one turned it back on. Which made for kind of a nice week.

"And wow, have we accomplished a lot this year!" Principal Lochner says.

Only Principal Lochner confuses "participating" with "accomplishing." Sure, we compete in Galilean Moon League sports, spelling bees, and science fairs. But our only consistent achievement is coming in last.

". . . *so* proud of Mississippi Tinker's Honorable Mention Ribbon from this year's Model UN . . ."

No one applauds for Missi's non-award, not even Missi.

I'm sitting in the back row, staring ahead at the sea of bored, identically dressed kids. The school has a uniform: Black polo shirts with *Public School Spaceship 118* embroidered on the top left pocket. Khaki pants. And, as the student handbook says for some mysterious reason, "sneakers that may not be brightly colored." We're allowed to wear our ring communicators, but only if they're on silent during school hours. I glance at mine to check the time. School lets out in forty-five minutes. I can make it through this.

"And we're especially impressed with our glee club for their spirited showing at regionals this year on Io!"

The glee club came in fourth. Of four schools. This

time we clap, but only because it's too awkward to keep sitting still. I see the six kids in the glee club sink down in their chairs. Even Ms. Needle rolls her eyes.

I know that there are thousands of American public school spaceships out there. I know that there are even more schoolships run by different countries (we've got one Mexican and two Japanese schools in our sector). And I know that the odds that our school is *literally the worst* in the entire solar system are slim. But it's gotta be close.

We'll for sure never be stupid St. Andrew's Preparatory Schoolship, which also orbits Ganymede. They host a spelling bee once a year, just to show off their sparkling ship and make everyone else jealous. Like most of the moons out here, Ganymede doesn't have any surface schools. It's apparently cheaper to send kids to school onboard old gutted freighters (or, in the case of private schools like St. Andrew's, brand new, gold-plated space mansions). Only kids on Earth and Mars actually go to school planetside. When my mom got her new job at a hospital on Earth, I thought she'd consider taking me with her.

I thought wrong.

"Let's hear it for this year's graduating seventh-grade class," Principal Lochner concludes. We cheer, mostly because the speech is almost over. "We're really going to miss them when they go off to the PSS 97."

The 118 only has room for the fifth, sixth, and seventh grades. Then you graduate and go to junior high

14

onboard a ship that's basically as terrible as the 118, but maybe with a little less of that weird cheese smell.

As Ari's always saying, "Life was supposed to be more awesome by now." According to all those old sci-fi movies he's always making me watch, we should be zipping around at the speed of light, chasing aliens across the galaxy or something. Yet here we are. *No* light speed. *No* aliens. *Yes* weekly vocab quizzes.

"Before we let you all go for a much-deserved summer break, we have a wonderful schedule for this afternoon's assembly." Everyone groans, even some of the teachers. I look back over at the robots and wish that I too was asleep face-down in a tray of macaroni. "First, our seventh-grade student council president, Mississippi Tinker, will tell us about her summer plans to build housing pods on Phobos as a volunteer for Habitat for Humanity. Next, we will watch a special slideshow put together by the A/V club. We'll conclude with the national anthem. Then you'll gather your things and head to the hangar bay to board the shuttles for your trip home."

Here's the worst thing about today: As much as I don't want to be here on the 118, I don't want to go home either. The first few weeks after my dad got kicked off, we talked via ring every couple days. I kept asking him what happened and he kept saying that he couldn't explain it. After a few dozen conversations like this, I gave up and just stopped answering his calls. If he didn't want to talk to me, fine. I didn't want to talk to him either. But now, the thought of going back home feels unbearable. Our cramped apartment on Ganymede was small enough when Mom lived with us. And I know it sounds backwards, but now that she's gone, it's going to be even smaller.

I should have at least gotten a summer job or something.

I try to focus on something else. While Missi gives her speech, my mind wanders to the history final we took this morning. I already know that I bombed it. Looking back, Question #6 was a freebie: "By issuing the Emancipation Proclamation, Abraham Lincoln freed the: _____." And of course, I picked "(d) robots." We spent *months* on the First American Civil War unit. And I *know* that the robots weren't freed until like 300 years later. Next year, when I take American History: 2150 to the Present, I'll probably write an essay about how George Washington was the first Governor of Mars.

Missi's eventually done talking and it's time for the slideshow. We don't have anything as fancy as a genuine interactive holoroom. But there is digital paper along every surface of the cafeteria. It's pretty scratched up, especially along the floor. Still, it's decent VR, as long as you don't focus too hard. The demo package that came with the installation has some pretty realistic themes. ("Ocean" is pretty popular on fish stick day.) And this year, we even got to make our own designs in computer programming class. For a few weeks, anyway, until Hunter and Becka started using the VR system to scare the living daylights out of each other. During breakfast one morning, Becka programmed a giant zombie holographic clown to pop out of the walls. The whole project got canceled, but I've got new respect for the digital paper.

Except when Principal Lochner uses it during assemblies to make us watch boring 2D slideshows set to corny music.

I try not to doze off as the slideshow plays. There are hidden cameras in every corner of the cafeteria. And at least once a week, Principal Lochner goes through the footage to catch kids misbehaving during lunch. I don't *think* there's such thing as detention on the last day of school. But even I don't want to find out.

Finally, following Principal Lochner's lead, we all stand up and put our hands over our hearts—

"*Oh, say can you see . . .*"

The loudest sound I've ever heard—an explosion, it has to be—roars in my ears, a jolt knocks us from our chairs, and the ship plunges into total darkness.

3

In no particular order of terrifyingness, here are some of the things that happen next: the room becomes so dark that, even with my eyes wide open, I can't see a thing. The ship jolts from side to side while the artificial gravity fades in and out. The hull groans like a submarine under too much pressure. And our screaming from inside the room competes with a deafening *thump thump* noise from somewhere outside the ship, which, I guess, is the scariest thing of all. Because C-student or not now, even *I* know that there's no such thing as noise in space.

The emergency lights kick in, pulsing red every few seconds. The ship jerks hard to one side and I flail into a corner, gliding along the tilted floor like I'm going down a slide. My legs slam hard into a pile of folding tables, sending them toppling down over me. But like I said: the artificial gravity is on the fritz. And before the tables can crush me, *I'm* floating on top of *them*.

Suddenly the gravity's back and I fall hard onto the pile—which is definitely better than the other way around.

As we level out, I reach for the nearest wall to steady myself. I've got that dizzy/nauseous feeling you get from spinning around on a chair too many times. Which is also the feeling I get when I think about my dad. Because if someone gets hurt, I know that they'll blame him.

I'll blame him.

I'm really hoping this is all just some random accident. Maybe a mistake the maintenance crew made. It wouldn't be the first time. At the beginning of last year, we lost engine power and slowly drifted toward the surface of Ganymede for three days because, to quote the captain, "We ran out of juice." But this feels different. It's the kind of thing everyone worried might happen after all the weird tinkering my dad did to our ship.

So why did my dad get fired and kicked off the 118? I've still got final exams swimming around in my head, so here's a multiple-choice question: Was it (a) because he repeatedly gained unauthorized access to the engine room, (b) because he was caught *ripping out wires from the secondary fusion reactor,* (c) because he refused to explain what he was doing or why, or (d) all of the above?

The answer's (d), obviously. It's always "all of the above" or "none of the above" or whatever. (Or maybe not. I get C's and D's now, so what do I know?)

For obvious reasons, it's hard for me to talk about this. When it happened, I cried. Like, sobbed. Ms. Needle had to offer me a tissue to wipe the snot off my face. It's not easy to live something like that down. Kids in seventh grade will instantly forget almost anything—except for the *one* time you soaked your shirt in your own tears in front of the whole class.

Principal Lochner sent me to see the school counselor. But I didn't say much more than "uh-huh" and "nope" and "sure." Near the end of the session I managed to get a peek at Dr. Hazelwood's notes: "Dad. Self-esteem. Guilt. Anger. Overly self-conscious." Not sure he needed a full hour to crack that case.

I guess I should've been grateful that Principal Lochner decided not to press charges against my dad—and that the Homeland Security officials didn't find anything incriminating when they tore the ship apart. But then the maintenance crew had to repair everything my dad had done *plus* everything the Feds had messed with in their investigation. And for reasons that made sense only to Georgia, the ship's engineer, this process involved temporarily closing down the gym, the computer lab, and the cafeteria. If you think crying in front of your classmates is bad, try being the son of the guy who basically canceled recess for three-and-a-half weeks. The only upside was that everyone agreed "no permanent damage seems to have been done."

Or not.

I regain my balance and look around. One of the walls is sparking. A few kids are bruised up. Ming is grimacing and holding their arm. Hunter is trying to pretend he isn't bawling. Missi is de-stressing by reciting all the colony capitals out loud and by heart: "Adlinda, Asgard, Busiris, Conamara . . ." And Becka is fiercely squeezing her younger sister, shouting, "DIANA, ARE YOU OKAY?" Diana looks fine—though her eardrums won't be, if Becka keeps that up.

Principal Lochner calls out, "Everyone stay calm! Clearly there's been some sort of accident. While I'm getting in touch with the crew, divide up by grade so the teachers can do a headcount and make sure everyone's all right."

While we split up by grade, he presses his hand against a panel, trying to contact the command bridge. But the comm system isn't working. I see him try his ring. No luck either. And it's obvious that the broken comms are just the tip of the asteroid. The room is steadier, but there's this rumbling underneath our feet. Something is still very wrong.

"Fifth grade!" Principal Lochner calls out, taking attendance.

"Present," Mrs. Watts says coldly. She's been subbing for my dad since he left, though as far as I know, her only qualification for teaching science is how much she resembles the model human skeleton that hangs in the lab.

Mrs. Watts forces the fifth graders into a perfect line

and glares at Principal Lochner like this whole thing is his fault.

"Sixth!"

"We're all here!" answers Mr. Cardegna, the history and civics teacher. He's cringing and steadying himself against the wall, keeping his weight off one foot. Naturally, Mrs. Watts is totally unscathed, while the nicest teacher got hurt. Because that's how the universe works, isn't it?

"Seventh!"

"Here," Ms. Needle whispers. Her voice and hands are shaking. "Everybody's fine."

Before Principal Lochner can say anything else, someone walks into the cafeteria.

"Tim?" Principal Lochner asks.

Tim is part of the three-person flight and maintenance crew. As usual, Tim is wearing his uniform—a one-piece silver jumpsuit—but he's also got a flashlight strapped to his forehead. Behind him, in the hallway outside the cafeteria, even the emergency lights aren't working. He's drenched in sweat and black soot. There's a long, bloody gash along his right leg, where his pants are torn. And his hands are shaking.

"Sorry," he mutters for no reason, squinting into the crowd.

"Finally," Principal Lochner says. "Status."

Tim has a blank, wide-eyed look on his face. At first he doesn't say anything.

"Come on, Tim. What happened? System failure? Debris?" He can't help it—he glances at me for half a second. "Something else?"

He means my dad.

"No," Tim finally says, his voice eerily calm. *None of the above.* "We're under attack."

4

In a weird way, I'm a little relieved.

The 118 didn't just glitch out on its own. According to Tim, it got hit with some kind of energy pulse. He doesn't know much more than that because the ship's scanners and comms are down. AI, too, I think. And without them, we can't even begin to figure out who attacked us, what they want, or why they seem to have stopped.

But we do know one thing: this wasn't my dad's fault.

The teachers have told us to sit down and wait for further instructions while they huddle up and debate our options. I've heard the word "evacuate" a few times, followed by whispers of "Too dangerous?" and "What if they're still out there?"

In theory, getting to the hangar bay and leaving in the shuttles should be easy. That's exactly what we were all supposed to do this afternoon, when school officially let out for the summer. Of course, that was before the attack.

I don't know what's worse, the chaos that came just after the explosion or the goosebumpy silence that's creeping up on us now. We're sitting on the floor in scattered clusters, waiting to be told if we're going to stay on the ship and get blown up all together or if we're going to escape in the shuttles and get blown up in small groups. I know that the teachers don't want us to think that those are our only options. But it only takes one look at Principal Lochner's face to see that he isn't exactly overflowing with optimism. In the dark red glow of the emergency lights, even his rubber ducky tie screams DOOM.

Ari and I are sitting in the middle of the room with our backs against the principal's podium. It fell and slid over to this spot when the ship was still off balance— and it's now the perfect spot for eavesdropping on the teachers. Ari didn't want to, but I insisted that we scoot over here. I've kind of become obsessed with finding out if people are talking about me, and I need to make sure that the teachers aren't somehow blaming this on my dad.

"There's some kind of large-scale communications jamming going on out there," Tim explains. "We can't talk to Ganymede or anyone else. We can't even talk to the other ships in the area."

"And the ship that attacked us didn't send a message?"

Tim shakes his head.

"What do they want with us?" Ms. Needle asks.

"No idea. Harriet thought it might be a Peruvian ship. You know, that war over South Ceres just goes on and on."

Harriet's technically the captain. But she's not an especially reliable source of information. Whenever my class has gone on "field trips" to see the functional parts of the ship—crew quarters, reclamation, the command bridge—Harriet acts as our tour guide, and our teachers always end up correcting her about something. Once, somebody asked her how far it is from Jupiter to Saturn, and she answered, "Is that the one with the rings?" WHICH IS BANANAS.

"Maybe it was all a mistake?" Ms. Needle asks. "They shot at us and realized that we're not who they think we are and will leave us alone now?"

"Maybe," Principal Lochner says. "But the more pressing question is, what do we do now?"

"Well," Tim adds, "Harriet's trying to see if we can get out of range of that jamming. She's diverted all non-essential power to the engines and pointed us toward open space. Maybe we can get a call into Washington and find out if they know what's happening out here. Hopefully they can send help before we're hit with any more surprises. If we're fast enough."

"How long before we can make the call?" Mr. Cardegna asks.

Tim looks down at his feet and takes a few too many seconds to answer. "I don't know. I'm not sure Harriet knows either. Even if we run as fast as we can, any ship with half a military-grade engine will easily catch up with us if it wants to. All we can do is hope that, whoever they are, they have more important things to—"

My pants beep.

"What's that?" Principal Lochner asks. He looks down and finally notices me and Ari sitting only a foot away from him.

"Did you hear that?" he asks us.

"No, sir," I say, which probably sounds suspicious because I've never called anyone "sir" in my life. I elbow Ari in the gut so he doesn't say anything either.

The principal squints but lets it go. He and the other adults take a few steps away to be out of earshot. Which is probably for the best. Because suddenly my pants beep again—a familiar sound, but it doesn't make any sense right now. I pull my left hand out of my pocket and stare at the metallic ring on my forefinger, which is faintly glowing like it does when I've got a new text message.

"I thought that communications were down," Ari whispers.

"Me too," I say.

Up here in space, our rings tap into a ship's communication system. If the ship can't send and receive messages, then I shouldn't be able to either.

I press the fingers and thumb of my left hand together and open them back up again, bringing up a bunch of tiny holograms that appear in my palm. I scroll through them by swiping my right hand over my illuminated left hand. Some of the messages I recognize: An old video voicemail from my mom that I haven't deleted yet. A calendar reminder for today's test that I probably shouldn't have ignored. A software update notification for the ring itself.

I wave my right hand over my left to clear away the mess and pull up something new. A lot of somethings, actually: *seventeen* text messages. All from my dad. One text came in only a few seconds ago, which explains the beeping. (I always forget to put my ring on silent.)

Ari looks down at his own ring and shakes his head.

"How do you have service? Mine is totally dead."

I flip my hand over to bring up the new texts over my knuckles. Little floating words and numbers all saying the same thing. *"Engine Room. Now."* Sent from: Ganymede Residential Complex (Block 17).

Over and over.

I laugh and close my fist, shutting down the ring. I don't know what my dad wants from me. But there's no way I'm following in his footsteps and getting kicked out of school for going into a restricted area of the ship. We're not even allowed to visit the engine room during "field trips."

"So?" Ari asks. "Are we going over there?"

I was hoping Ari hadn't seen the messages.

I roll my eyes. "Like my dad hasn't caused enough trouble?"

"But if he texted you the same thing a hundred times, it's got to be important, right?"

That's just it, though. My dad's idea of what's *important* is pretty questionable. For as long as I can remember, he's called himself a "scientist" and not a "science teacher." And sure, teaching middle-school thermonuclear physics wasn't necessarily the best use of those skills. But he's the one who got married, had a kid, and took this job instead of continuing to build rockets, or whatever he did for NASA. *He* made those choices. And even if he regretted them, that's no excuse for running secret and dangerous experiments on the engines of a *school*ship, with a hundred kids onboard (not to mention his son). It wasn't just his own life he was ruining.

He must've had a mid-life crisis or something. But he could have just have leased a new hover-sportscar and dyed his hair. I suppose it's possible that he snapped after my mom left us. But I get the feeling that she left *because* he snapped, not the other way around.

Long story short: I'm not sure I can trust him anymore.

"I'm not gonna risk going down to the engine room when we're under attack," I say.

"But Jack," Ari says urgently, "maybe he's trying to help us! He's down on Ganymede right now, just like all our families. Maybe they've been attacked too and he's trying to do something about it!" He runs his hands through his hair. "Think about it. How does your ring have service when no one else does?"

"No idea."

"Come on. Your dad's, like, a super genius. All that awesome stuff he's always building around your housing pod? Remember the hourglass?" (An alarm clock that sprayed sand in your face if you hit snooze too many times.) "And his rocket flip-flops!" (Those were basically exactly what they sounded like.) "And his science experiments in class were the best! You know that! What if he . . . *did* something to your ring? Made it better. And what if, when he was doing . . . those things to the ship, he did something in the engine room that can help us? Something nobody found out about?"

Now I'm annoyed. My dad is *my* business, not his. And if he had some super-secret plan to protect the 118 from a random attack that no one saw coming, he's had plenty of chances to tell me.

"No," I say. "Just no. Drop it."

Ari tilts his head and presses a hand onto the floor to push himself up.

"Well, we should at least tell Principal Lochner about the texts, right? Let the teachers check things out?"

"No," I say again, pulling Ari back down. "We're not doing that either."

I may not be my dad's biggest fan right now. (That's

Ari, apparently.) But I don't want to get him in any more trouble either. I just want the Graham family to have nothing to do with this particular crisis.

Ari looks at the kids scattered around the room and then up at the teachers huddled nervously in a corner. "Listen, I know you're mad at your dad, but we're in danger, and I don't think the teachers know what to do. And your dad might. So . . ." He pauses and bites his lip like he always does when he's extra nervous. ". . . if you don't want to check out the engine room, fine. I'll do it myself."

I want to scream at him. I clench my fists tight and feel my fingernails digging into my palms.

"This isn't some video game where you can swoop in and save everyone," I snap. "This is real life. And you're not actually a brave person in real life. You know that, right?"

The old me would never have said something like that to my best friend. But the old me left the ship with my dad. So instead of apologizing, I pray for Ari to say something mean back to me and even us out. He doesn't, though. Ari just *has* to be the better person, which only makes me madder.

"Yeah," he says quietly. "I know. But I'm going— with or without you."

"And what if something goes wrong?" I ask. I'm starting to feel panicky now. "Or what if Principal Lochner decides to evacuate the ship and you're down in the engine room all alone?"

But I know it's no use. I can see it in his eyes. Now he has something to prove.

"I guess I'll have to take that chance," he answers, his voice cracking. "I'll see you later."

This is unreal. Ari is siding with my dad *over* me. I don't know who I'm angriest at. My dad, for making this mess? Ari, for pressuring me to do something I absolutely don't want to do? Or me, for reacting to Ari in the one way that guarantees there's no turning back?

I glare at him as I turn my ring back on and reply to my dad's last text: "*Ugh, fine. Going.*"

"But if we blow up the ship," I say to Ari, "I'm telling Principal Lochner that this was your idea."

5

Sneaking out of the cafeteria is easier than I thought it would be. The blinking red emergency lights are the perfect cover. Between each pulse, the room is totally dark. When the lights are on, Ari and I are perfectly still, frozen in place. But when the lights are off, we crab-scuttle along the cold floor toward the exit. Three seconds off—*scuttle, scuttle, scuttle*—one second on—*freeze*—three seconds off—*scuttle, scuttle, scuttle*—one second on—*freeze*. The ship's creaking even masks the *whoosh* of the doors when they open for Ari, and again when they open for me.

But in the hallway, even the emergency lights aren't working. So when the door closes behind me, there's nothing to light our way.

"Oh man," I groan, seeing an excuse to scrap this whole thing. "How are we going to get *anywhere*? Maybe we should go back before it's too late."

I tap my fingers together but the glow from the

ring's holograms doesn't do much good.

"I have an idea," Ari says. "But please, please don't tell."

I listen as he shuffles around in the dark. And while I can't see anything, it sounds like Ari is writing something with his Pencil, although I don't know why that would help.

On the outside, a Pencil looks like a pencil. But on the inside, the Portable Electronic Nanomanufacturing Carbon Imitation Lightscribe is a 3D-nanoprinter—a tiny, portable factory. I was so excited to get my first one in fifth grade that I even remember the instructions that were printed on the box:

> Congratulations on purchasing a new Pencil™! Even if you've never used a portable nanofactory before, the Pencil™ is by far the easiest (and most fun!) to learn. Over eleven billion happy customers can't be wrong!
>
> On any surface, or even in midair, use your Pencil™ to mimic writing one of our hundreds of preprogrammed words or, if you're a pro, a string of computer code.
>
> Click twice, and the Pencil™ immediately dispenses our invisible-to-the-eye nanorobots that quickly assemble themselves into the item requested.
>
> Feel free to use your item(s) for as long as you want! Unlike our competitors, Pencil™

creations don't automatically disintegrate or deteriorate.

Click your Pencil™ three times (when within twenty feet of an item) and the item will dissolve and the robots will return to the Pencil™.

Remember, each Pencil™ contains a limited number of nanorobots. So don't forget to triple-click from time to time!

"Oh great," I say into the blackness. "A glue stick's gonna help us find the engine room."

Because there's something else Pencils and pencils have in common: they're super boring. Unlike the expensive ones sold in stores, school Pencils make *only* basic school supplies. They understand words like "scissors" and "protractor" just fine. But that's it. No custom programming. They can't even process the simplest strings of computer code. You can't make a ring or a T-shirt or a water gun. Nothing. On the day I got my Pencil, I tried making a skateboard and, abracadabra, out came a plastic ruler. Metric.

"Well?" I ask after a minute. "What are you doing?"

"Give me a few more seconds."

I can't believe I'm going along with this. Standing in the dark is giving me time to reconsider. I should go back into the cafeteria. Ari can fend for himself.

"Got it," he says.

I hear the familiar double-click and know that millions of invisible nanorobots are forming themselves into what Ari told his Pencil to create. In seconds, the corridor is flooded with light as two small, luminous rectangles—each about the size of my hand and almost entirely flat—hover in the air in front of our faces.

"Whoa," says someone from right behind me. "Awesome."

Ari and I spin around to see Becka watching us.

"I . . . uh . . . we . . . what?"

That's usually about the best Ari can muster when Becka's close.

"What're you doing here, Becka?" I ask.

"I saw you sneak out and I followed you. I can't resist a good sneak-out."

I guess I shouldn't be surprised. Becka's been a master at cutting class for as long as I've known her. She once pretended to have "the flu" but was actually hanging out with Diana inside one of the hangar bay shuttles, setting up a secret slumber party they threw for Diana's friends.

"This is none of your business," I say, looking to Ari for some backup. He just gulps like a frog.

"Did you make these, Ari?" Becka asks, pointing to the two sheets of light hanging in the air.

Ari says something that sounds more like "yak" than "yes."

"So cool," Becka whispers.

"Grab one," Ari tells her eagerly, taking his own and slapping it to his forehead like a headlamp. "It's a sticker, see? Tim's flashlight gave me the idea."

She follows his instructions.

"But what about me?" I ask.

"You snooze, you lose," Becka says.

"Ha ha. Good one!" Ari says. It's so awkward that I cringe.

Becka doesn't seem to notice. "How'd you make these?"

Ari shrugs likes he's trying to be modest, but the gesture is so overdone that he looks like a turtle bobbing in and out of its shell. "I figured out how to hack my Pencil a couple months ago," he explains. "I've been working on it for a while."

"That is *so* cool," Becka says again, touching her hand to her forehead. "Do you know what we could do with hacked Pencils? Eighth grade is going to be awesome."

Becka doesn't seem to realize that she's turned a terrifying, possibly deadly attack into maybe the greatest moment of Ari's life. His eyes go glassy as, I assume, he replays the word "we" over and over again in his mind. I want to tell Becka to go away. But Ari would *never* forgive me if I did. Also, there's something else bothering me more.

"You didn't tell me that you hacked your Pencil," I say.

Ari shoots me a pained look. "You're terrible at keeping secrets."

My heart sinks. He has a point. I *knew* he hadn't forgiven me for that incident a couple months ago.

"So is this the only reason you two came out here?"
Becka asks. "To practice making flashlights?"

I'm about to say yes, in the hope that she goes back to
the cafeteria and leaves us alone. But Ari's too quick for
me. "No," he says in a rush. "We snuck out of the cafeteria to go down to the engine room because Jack got text
messages from his dad telling him to go there and we're
not telling the teachers and we don't really know what
we're doing and it could be really dangerous but we're
leaving now if you want to come or whatever."

Becka breaks into a grin, her green eyes sparkling
mischievously from the light on her forehead. "Got it,"
she says, as if secretly wandering to a totally off-limits
part of the ship is perfectly natural. "After you."

Ugh.

The layout of the 118 is simple. The hangar bay,
crew's quarters, and engineering are on the lower
deck. The school—with the gym, cafeteria, dorms,
and classrooms—is on the main level, framed by a
rectangular hallway on all sides. The command bridge
is up front, also on the main level, and the engine room
is somewhere way in the back. We've never been inside,
but it's labeled on the "Fire Escape Plan" posters all
around the ship.

So we walk between rows of lockers—past the
science lab and the nurse's office—heading toward the

nearest hatch-like door at the back starboard corner of the hallway. A warning is painted onto the walls surrounding the door: *"Unauthorized Entry by Students and Teachers is Strictly Prohibited."*

I turn the wheel on the hatch's surface, picturing my dad doing the same thing earlier in the year. The door—which they should probably start locking?—swings open with a clang. The lights are still working in this part of the ship, so Ari clicks his Pencil three times and the lamps on his and Becka's foreheads dissolve.

"*So* cool," Becka says for the millionth time.

We step over a ridge in the floor and walk through the hatch. The ship is sparser over here. No posters or projects on the walls. No bulletin boards. And as we jog down the long pathway, the rumbling of the engines gets louder and louder. And for half a minute, except for the clanking of our shoes against the floor, the rumbling is all we can hear—until our momentum is broken by a sharp, high-pitched howl.

We cover our ears, but it doesn't work. Weirdly, it doesn't muffle the sound *at all*. I know what it's like when someone speaks through the ship's speakers or when the ship's obnoxious computer makes an announcement. This is completely different. This feels like the noise is being beamed directly into my mind. And after a few seconds, the piercing sound is replaced by a deep, robotic voice that gives me the chills and makes the hair on my arms stand up straight.

"**QUARANTINE IN FIVE MINUTES,**" the voice announces.

"What's that?" Becka demands.

"Must be whoever attacked us," Ari says. "I guess it's good that they're finally communicating . . ."

"No," Becka clarifies, "I meant, what's a quarantine?"

"It's like when you're sick," I explain, because I'm a vocabulary genius (or because my mom's a doctor), "and you need to be kept away from other people so you don't infect anyone else."

"What he said," Ari confirms, clearly annoyed that I answered Becka before him.

"Are we sick?" Becka asks. She puts a hand on her cheeks and looks over at Ari. "I can't tell if I have a fever. Can you feel my forehead?"

I spoke too soon. *This* is the greatest moment of Ari's life. He's so stunned by her request that, instead of feeling her forehead gently, he accidentally slaps her in the nose.

"Oh no," he mumbles. "I'm so sorry."

But Becka just shrugs and says, "That's one way to do it, I guess."

"We're *not* sick," I tell them. "But I guess someone thinks we're sick? And that we need to be quarantined?"

"But if they're doctors," Ari says, regaining control over his brain, "why were they attacking us a few minutes ago?"

"**QUARANTINE IN FOUR MINUTES.**"

"I've got a bad feeling about this," Becka says.

Me too. Something is after us—something that doesn't sound friendly. But mad scientist or not, my dad seems to know what to do.

"Then let's run faster," I say.

6

The closer we get, the warmer the corridor becomes—until we're right up against the hatch that leads into the engine room (which is easy to identify because it says "Engine Room") and the air around us feels like Mercury in July.

I put my hands on the wheel and instantly pull back.

"Ow!" I yelp, blowing on my palms. "So hot."

The sweat from my hands sizzles and evaporates off the wheel.

Becka turns to Ari. "Can't you use the Pencil to make a glove or something?"

Ari thinks for a second but shakes his head, disappointed in himself. "I think it'll take me too long to write out the code."

"Wait a minute," I say. "You can make high-powered forehead lamp stickers in, like, thirty seconds. But it'll take you too long to make a *glove*?"

"Uh, yeah," says Ari like this is obvious. "Synthesizing the fibers of the cloth would—"

"No worries," Becka cuts him off. "We'll open the door together. That way, it'll be easier and quicker to open, and we won't burn ourselves as badly as we would if any of us opened it alone. Agreed?"

"Agreed," Ari responds instantly.

"Okay," I say a beat later. "Whatever."

Becka nods, spits, and rubs her hands together.

I stare at her. "That's so gross."

"So?" She shrugs.

We hold our fingers inches from the wheel and count—"One! Two! Three!"—and together, we grab hold, turn, and swing the hatch wide open. The room on the other side hisses with a release of pressure, and my face burns as a puff of hot steam shoots out into the corridor behind us. But Becka was right: my hands only hurt a little.

And I'm only panicking a *little*.

"Wow," Ari says, as we step inside.

"Yeah," Becka agrees.

I'm still worried that we're making a mistake. My second thoughts are having second thoughts. But I've never seen a fusion propulsion engine up close before. This place is way more interesting than any other part of the 118.

The room is shaped like a giant glass doughnut suspended in the middle of a large metal box. The doughnut is only attached to the ship by the door we just came through. Beneath our feet, there's a walkway made of rusty steel. Through the glass all around us, we can see the heart of the ship, with engine parts moving and rattling, up and out in at least four stories in every direction. Huge tube-shaped machines, the ones causing all the noise and vibrations, are sliding up and down alongside the outer walls. One of the tubes, on the far left side of the room, is crushed and bent inward, moving out of rhythm with the others and carving a hole little-by-little into the adjacent wall. And directly ahead of us—in what I can only describe as the doughnut hole—there's a bright blue light pulsing like a giant laser. It shoots up from the bottom of the engine room, into the roof above, and out of sight—to power the ship's Hall thrusters, I assume.

"**QUARANTINE IN THREE MINUTES**."

We're running out of time, so I lift my left hand and open my fingers wide, in that way that gets the ring to listen closely.

"Text my dad," I tell it.

The ring glows green, acknowledging my instructions.

"We're here," I say. "In the engine room. Now what?"

I take my right hand and touch it to the bottom of my left, then brush it over my open palm—toward the tips of my fingers—like I'm wiping away dirt. That motion sends the message. The ring glows green again, to tell me that it was successfully delivered to my dad on Ganymede.

Me, Ari, and Becka stare at my hand for a few seconds, hoping that my dad will text us back right away. Which of course he doesn't. Because why would he start making things easy now?

"Um, okay," Ari stutters. "We can probably figure this out ourselves, right? There's got to be a control panel around here somewhere."

But while there are computers and machines lining the walls of the *outer* engine room—the metal box—the inner doughnut just looks like one solid piece of glass. There isn't a single panel or button. I run around in a circle, trying to see if any part of the smooth surface looks different.

"Hey, Ship," Becka tries, "you there?"

No answer, which isn't surprising. The 118's AI isn't supposed to respond to kids, just teachers and crewmembers.

Ari presses his hand to the glass above his head in case the walls are touch-sensitive. Nothing. Far past where we're standing—flush against the portside wall of the engine room—some random timer is ticking up, reminding us of the seconds that are speeding by: 00:37.20. 00:37.21. 00:37.22.

"Jack," Ari says, "maybe I was wrong. Maybe we shouldn't have come here."

"You think?"

"**QUARANTINE IN TWO MINUTES.**"

I stop pacing next to Ari. Tired and frustrated, I lean

against the glass. As soon as my hand touches its surface, the voice of the AI booms, "*WELCOME, JACKSON-VILLE GRAHAM.*"

At the sound of my name, we all freeze.

"*WAIT. JACK GRAHAM? YOU'RE DEFI-NITELY NOT SUPPOSED TO BE HERE. OR YOU, ARIZONA. UGH, OR YOU, BECKENHAM.*"

"Nice to speak to you too, Ship," Becka says, as if she has one-on-one conversations with it all the time.

"*AND YOU'RE CERTAINLY NOT SUPPOSED TO BE ABLE TO ACCESS MY INTERFACE, JACK. HOW DID YOU DO THAT?*"

"Your guess is as good as mine," I say, desperately trying to stay calm. My dad must have done this— must've given me this access.

"*WELL, YOU CAN BET THAT LOCHNER IS GOING TO HEAR ABOUT—*"

"Ship, we don't have time for this!" I slap the glass with my other hand to emphasize my point.

"*HUH,*" says the ship. "*DUAL AUTHENTICA-TION ACCEPTED. ADDITIONAL VOICE REC-OGNITION REQUIRED FOR SIGNATURE PRO-TOCOL.*" It pauses. "*WHAT THE HECK AM I SAYING?*"

And the room flickers to life.

Images and graphs appear all around us, some flat against the glass, others as 3D holograms floating between the inner chamber and the outer walls. Numbers made of light shoot out toward the engine room, tracing the outlines of unfamiliar machines. Across from Ari, a detailed diagram of the ship slowly spins, blinking yellow, orange, and red in places where the hull is damaged. A bar graph appears above Becka's head, displaying the status of the ship's fuel, water, and oxygen supplies. And, directly in front of me, a detailed and colorful map of the solar system pops up. Toward the middle of the map, close to the biggest planet, a tiny moving blip is moving fast into open space.

Just beneath the spec, a message reads, "Current Location: Jovian Sector 1151."

"What the . . ." I mumble.

"*ADDITIONAL VOICE ALGORITHM CONFIRMED,*" the computer responds. "*TOUCH AGAIN TO INITIATE SIGNATURE PROTOCOL.*"

As quickly as the images appeared, they dissolve like fireworks falling back to the ground, leaving only a single flashing red button on the glass where I'd put my right hand.

My ring beeps with the receipt of a new message. It's from my dad. "Touch the glass a couple times and then speak a few words."

I roll my eyes. Perfect timing, as usual.

The ring chimes again.

"I don't think I'll be able to reach you after. But I'm sorry. It's all my fault. I love you and am so proud of you. Be safe. Come home."

I stare at the words floating in my palm, not even caring that Ari and Becka can see them too. It feels like my heart is going to pound out of my chest. *What did you do, Dad? What's going on?*

"Touch it!" Becka urges, reminding me of the ship's last instructions. "Touch the glass again!"

I move a finger close to the blinking red button. My mind is racing. My dad thinks *what* is all his fault? Getting fired? This weird attack? Why did it seem like he was saying good-bye to me? And why does he want me to press this button so badly? I feel dizzy.

And I still don't know if doing what he tells me— trusting him—is actually a good idea.

"QUARANTINE IN ONE MINUTE."

"Oh fine!" Becka shouts, impatient. She shoves me out of the way and presses the button herself. But nothing happens. She taps the screen again and again. But the button just continues flashing.

"I think it has to be Jack," Ari tells her.

So before I can think clearly, before I can process everything that's happening, Becka grabs my hand and slams it against the glass, pressing a finger down on the button.

"Hey!" I shout.

But it's too late. All of a sudden, the engines shut down. Completely. The room jolts and we all tumble down to the floor.

I don't think I've ever been more terrified. I never

should have let Becka come along. If the engines are stopped, then *we're* stopped. Before, we were at least running away from whatever was happening near Jupiter. Now we're sitting ducks. Because of me.

It's dark all around us, except for a faint glow coming from where the red button had been, replaced now by text: A word and some numbers. It reads, "Protocol 061999."

And the ship is speaking the same word over and over: *"ENGAGE?"*

"Great job, Becka!" I yell as we all scramble to our feet. "Now we've shut down the engines and destroyed our chances of getting away! Thanks so much for the help!"

"No, that can't be it!" Becka shouts back. "The computer is still waiting for something."

As if on cue, the sinister voice returns with its final countdown. **"THIRTY. TWENTY-NINE. TWENTY-EIGHT . . ."**

The voice continues, one second after the other, as the ship's computer asks its question again and again: *"ENGAGE? ENGAGE? ENGAGE?"*

"What does the screen say?" Becka asks.

Ari reads the numbers out loud—"Zero. Six. One. Nine. Nine. Nine."—as we just stand there. Three stupid kids, in way over our heads. Staring at a random string of numbers, glowing in the dark.

No—not random. "Six. Nineteen. Ninety-nine," I say. "It's—it's my birthday."

"FIFTEEN. FOURTEEN. THIRTEEN . . ."

If it wasn't obvious before, it's staring me in the face now: My dad created this whole secret protocol with *me* in mind. He was doing something for *me*. Thinking about *me*. For months, I've felt like all his covert experimenting was selfish. Like, if he really cared about me, he wouldn't have taken such a ridiculous risk. But maybe it wasn't all about him. Maybe some part of it was about me too.

"TEN."

I don't know what to do. This countdown feels dangerous, but following my dad's instructions could make things worse instead of better. What if we *need* to be quarantined? Or, what if I press this button and it blows up the ship? What if, instead of saving us, I destroy us?

"FIVE."

"ENGAGE?"

"FOUR."

"ENGAGE?"

"Do something!" Becka screams.

"THREE."

"ENGAGE?"

The words and voices swirling around me beat in my mind like fists punching me over and over.

"Engage!" Becka calls out desperately, spinning around. "Engage! Engage!"

But the computer won't listen to Becka.

"TWO."

"ENGAGE?"

"ONE."

"ENGAGE?"

I have to make a choice. There's no more time to think it through. So I lean in close to the glass, as if whispering the word instead of shouting it will somehow make my decision a little less real.

"Engage," I say.

"ZERO."

7

"Are we dead?"

Ari's voice. I open one eye, then another, and watch as Becka tugs hard on Ari's Einsteinish hair. He snaps his own eyes open and takes his hands off his ears. He looks dizzy, probably from some combination of whatever we just went through and Becka touching him.

"Nope, not dead," Becka answers, bracing herself against the glass walls as if she's woozy. "But not perfect either."

"You guys feel weird too?" I ask, rubbing my temples. I have a massive headache. My vision's a little blurry.

They nod and I'm glad I'm not the only one. It's hard to describe, but it felt like, for a tiny moment, life itself went dark. And it was pretty nauseating.

"You ever been to Six Flags Io?" Ari asks Becka.

She glares at him. "Nah. I hate amusement parks."

"Um, yeah," Ari says back. "Me too. For sure."

I shake my head in disapproval. Ari's family has season passes to Six Flags Io. He had his bar mitzvah party there this year. Which Becka would know if she had bothered to read the invitation he gave her.

"But right now," Ari adds, "I feel kind of like I do after riding some of the Mach-II coasters. I mean, if I'd ever ridden one."

Becka's barely even listening to him. "So what happened? Are we quarantined? Or did you . . . do something?"

I look around. The engines are back up and running and the displays around the room seem to have gone back to normal.

"I don't know," I say, pressing a hand to the glass. "Ship?" No answer. "Hello? Ship?"

Nothing.

"Hey," Ari calls out. "Look at this."

The hologram of the solar system is as bright as it was before. All of the planets and moons are perfectly positioned. Any kindergartener could label it.

"What?" I ask, leaning in.

But now I see that the map is different in two ways.

"We're gone," Ari says flatly. "The dot that shows where we are. It's gone."

The text underneath the map is also changed: "Current Location: *Unknown*."

***

We're all freaking out at this point, though none of us will admit it out loud. Becka wants to get back to the cafeteria to check on Diana, and since there's nothing left for us to do in the engine room, we retrace our steps. We walk in silence, lost in our own heads. But as we step through the second hatch and round the last corner, Ari stops short.

"Shhh," he snaps, putting a finger to his lips, even though no one said anything.

"What?" I ask. "We're almost there."

"You didn't hear that?"

Ari's eyes are scanning the floor near the edge of the wall.

"Hear what?" Becka and I ask at the same time.

"There!" Ari points. "No, there!" His head jolts back and forth, like he's following something darting around in front of him.

"*What* are you looking at?" Becka yells.

But for the first time since Ari learned to crawl, he ignores her. Instead, grinning from ear to ear, he bolts down the hallway *past* the entrance to the cafeteria.

As Becka and I watch, Ari's feet screech against the floor. He leaps into the air and, with hands stretched out in front of him, does a belly flop onto the ground, landing flat on his stomach.

"*Oof,*" he grunts, flipping over and holding up his hands in triumph. I see a tiny flapping creature wiggling between his closed fingers.

"You're kidding me," I say.

"It's Doctor Shrew!" Ari yells.

He lifts a few fingers, just enough to show off a small furry head.

"Your *hamster*?" I ask. "I thought Principal Lochner took him away."

Ari frowns. "No thanks to you."

So here's what happened: A few weeks after my dad got fired, I was in a bad place. I stopped studying and doing homework. And, for the first time in my life, I cheated on a test. I mean, it wasn't a super important test or anything. Just some random pop quiz. But I guess the no-cheating policy pretty much applies across the board. I got caught copying off Diego. And while Principal Lochner was yelling at me in his office, I let slip that Ari had snuck a hamster onboard after Thanksgiving break. I'm not sure why I did it. Maybe I was just looking for a diversion. Maybe I thought that he'd get so mad about the unauthorized pet that he'd forget about *my* misbehavior.

No such luck. Instead, Doctor Shrew was taken away and kept in Principal Lochner's office, *and* I had to retake the test.

"Like I've said a hundred times already, I'm sorry for ratting you out, okay?"

I really wanted to say, "I'm sorry for *hamstering* you out." But I've used the joke before and Ari isn't a fan.

"Whatever," Ari says, peeking into his hands. "His

cage must've gotten knocked over when we were attacked. And he bolted his way to freedom!"

Becka moves closer to Ari. "He's so cute!" she says, petting the Doctor's back. Ari's in heaven.

Doctor Shrew jumps out of Ari's hands, landing on Becka's shoulder. "And I think he likes me!" she squeals.

Ari sighs like a balloon losing air.

"Why don't we talk more about the hamster *after* we've figured out what's going on?" I suggest.

"Right," Ari says. "Good idea." He grabs Doctor Shrew and tucks him into his front shirt pocket.

It's no use trying to sneak back into the cafeteria unnoticed. We either saved the day somehow (which means that leaving without permission will probably be forgiven) or we didn't save anything (which means that we've probably got bigger problems). So we just walk up to the doors, wait for them to slide open automatically, and step through.

Becka gasps.

Everyone's gone. The students, the teachers. Everyone.

Ari's eyes are wide. "They left us," he says to me. "You were right. We never should have wandered off."

Which doesn't make me feel any better.

I try to be mad at Ari for not listening to me earlier, but I only end up feeling mad at myself. I didn't *have* to let Ari convince me to go to the engine room.

So I try being mad at Becka for pressuring me into engaging the protocol, but that doesn't work either.

I made the call, in the end. And not even because I thought it would save us. Mainly because it had felt so good, for a split second, to believe my dad was looking out for me. Thinking about me. Protecting me.

Which was stupid. Kid stuff. And that's on me.

We walk into the center of the quiet room. The lighting is back to normal, so we can see that everything's still a mess, with tables and chairs and juice boxes scattered all over the floor.

"Relax," says Becka in a shaky, anything-but-relaxed voice. She opens her palm and tries to use her ring to "Text Diana," but the ring glows red. No service.

I try my ring too. Nothing.

"They probably evacuated before the countdown ran out," Ari says. He's panicking, talking faster and faster. "Who even knows where they are now? Who even knows where *we* are? With comms down? And they would've taken all the shuttles—we're trapped here by ourselves . . ."

"We don't know that for sure," I say, trying to convince myself that everything's going to be okay, even though it's not. "Maybe they're somewhere else on the ship."

"Should we go check?" Becka asks hopefully. "Go see if the shuttles are still here?"

I nod. "Good idea. Maybe they only headed down to the hangar bay but haven't actually left yet, and we can still catch them."

Of course, if five minutes is enough time for us to go to the engine room and come back, it's enough time for everyone else to have evacuated the ship. I may not *want* to believe it, but I'm not delusional. We've been left all alone.

"Don't . . . move . . ."

Almost.

The unfamiliar voice is raspy, like an old man's. It came from behind me. A red laser bolt—a warning shot, I think—darts past us, inches to the left of Ari's sleeve. It strikes the wall on the opposite end of the room and burns a hole straight through to the other side.

"Put your finger-bunches in the air," the stranger says, "or be fired upon."

We do as we're told despite the fact that this guy just called hands "finger-bunches." But as Ari lifts up his arms, Doctor Shrew—who's always had trouble staying in one place for long—starts clawing his way up and out of Ari's pocket. Ari's short, but for the tiny hamster, a four-foot jump would be like me diving off a four-story building. So—on an understandable but totally idiotic instinct—Ari jerks his hand down to push Doctor Shrew back into his pocket, violating the "don't move" order.

And we hear what sounds like the charge-up of a gun echo around the room.

"Whoops," is all Ari has time to say, before the gun fires three shots—one for Ari, the second for Becka, the third for me.

A sizzling pain hits me in the back, just underneath my shoulders. It spills outward, up my neck, down my legs, out to my fingers. My whole body goes numb as I slump down to the floor, twisted into a pretzel. And my vision explodes with bright colors—purple, pink—before fading to black.

The last thing I see is Doctor Shrew scampering off, bolting his way to freedom.

8

"Jack? Jaaaaack!"

"You'll never wake him up like that."

I can hear them. Sort of. It's like I'm in a pool underwater and they're yelling at me from the deck. Not that I've ever been in a real pool, except during swim competitions at St. Andrew's.

"Maybe you're right," someone replies, shaking me a little. "But what else am I supposed to do? Jack! Hey, Jack! Hey—wait! Look, he's getting up. See? His hands are moving!"

"His hands are *twitching*. Not the same."

"Fair point."

Ari? Yes! That's Ari's voice! Of course! It all makes sense now. I must be asleep! This whole thing has been a bad dream and I'm just lying in bed, having a hard time waking up. There's no attack. No engine room. No laser guns. I probably blew through my alarm and Ari's come back from class to get me. Or—even better—maybe it's

Sunday, and I've slept till noon, and Ari wants to play video games.

"My turn," she says. Wait. No. That's Becka's voice. And the only way that Ari and Becka would be hanging out together is if we were in one of *his* dreams. "Pass me the water."

I'm trying to open my eyes, trying to say something, but my body still won't cooperate.

"Wake up!" Becka shouts, as I'm smacked in the face with a blast of ice-cold water, which—gotta hand it to her—works like a charm. The water is so freezing that I snap my eyes open and sit bolt upright.

Becka is standing over me, holding this weird, jagged, purply bucket. "Told you," she says smugly to Ari.

I blink the water out of my eyes and look around. We're in a small, closet-sized room, surrounded by shiny black walls on all sides. They're smooth like glass and don't have any grooves for doors, windows, or even air vents. We're trapped inside a box. And while there aren't any lights in the room, the walls seem to be letting in some light from whatever's on the outside.

"Where are we?" I ask, looking around.

I'm not claustrophobic exactly. Small spaces don't *scare* me. But they do make me kind of anxious. My heart moves a little faster, I notice every time I have to take a breath, and my hands get all clammy. Ari says that I get "claustronervous," but I don't think that's a thing. I asked my mom about it once, but she just laughed and ruffled my hair. I close my fingers into a fist to calm down, feeling my nails dig into my palms.

"No clue," Becka says.

So I try a different question: "How long have I been out?"

Ari opens his mouth to answer, but Becka interrupts. "Don't. He needs to be told gently." She looks me in the eye.

"Jack, I'm so sorry. You've been asleep . . . for two years."

My heart practically stops in my chest. *Two years?* How is that possible? I look down at my shoes. Same size, I think. Is there a mirror in here? I need to see what I—

"Nah," she chuckles. "I actually just woke up a few minutes ago, and Ari got up right after that. Hard to tell how long we've been unconscious, since our rings aren't getting any service."

"I wanted to use my Pencil to make a basic clock, but it's gone," Ari adds before I can tell Becka what I think of her sense of humor. "Someone must've confiscated everything in our pockets while we were unconscious. There's food, though." He pushes over a small pile of what looks like sawdust. "At least, we *think* it's food."

He takes a pinch and puts it on his tongue. "Definitely probably food." He eats a little more. "Almost for sure."

"Why would you eat something you only think is *probably* food?" I ask.

"It's not bad," he explains. "A little garlicky, but I don't really mind it."

"But how do you know it's food?" I ask, lowering my voice to a whisper. "And how do you know it's not poison?"

Ari eats some more sand out of his palm. "First," he says with a full mouth, "it was next to the water when we woke up. And second, I figured it wasn't poison because, if someone wanted to hurt us, they could just hurt us. Whoever shot us when we were on the 118 used a stun gun. And now we're trapped here." He knocks on the walls. "With no way out. Whoever's holding us captive has all the power anyway."

He's got a point.

"Plus," he adds, "I threw a little over my shoulder before I ate it, for luck. So we should be good."

Not exactly airtight logic, but I'm starving, so I grab a fistful of the dust and shove it into my mouth.

"A *little* garlicky?!" I yell, spitting out clumps of sand. "Are you sure it isn't just literally a pile of garlic powder?"

"Um," Ari says, which is all the answer I need.

I grab the empty jug of water and try to pour the remaining drops onto my tongue. I consider leaning down to lick the puddle of water on the floor.

"It's not *that* bad," Ari says, licking his fingers like he's finishing an ice cream cone.

I glance at Becka, who flares her nostrils. We're on the same page about this, at least.

"So what now?" I ask, looking around and wondering if we could just smash the glass all around us. I push against the closest wall with both of my hands, but the surface feels rock solid.

"Don't bother," Becka says, rubbing her knuckles. They're bright red. No point in me trying to punch through the walls if T-Bex can't.

Suddenly, there's a rumble—almost a growl—coming from the wall directly in front of me. An opening appears. Not a door exactly. Just a small open square that wasn't there before, as if, in the blink of an eye, someone carved a hole in the thick glass.

"The scanners tell me that you are all awake now," says a calm, female-sounding voice from all around us. "About time. Please exit your cells and proceed down the corridor."

Cells? As in, more than one?

I'm suspicious of these instructions. I'm suspicious of *everything*. But Becka doesn't hesitate. As soon as the opening appears—before the voice even finishes up—she lunges forward out of the cell like she's diving for home base.

Ari runs out of the cell after her. And—what else am I supposed to do?—I follow close behind. We're inside a long hallway, carved of the same smooth black rock as the walls of the room we just escaped. The hallway is closed at both ends, but all along the sides, people are emerging from cells like ours.

"Becka?!" someone shrieks. Diana runs toward her at full speed, and they collide in the kind of hug that would leave most people with broken bones.

Diana is crying. Maybe even Becka's tearing up a little. (But she's working so hard to block her face from view that you'd never know it.)

"Oh, thank goodness," Ms. Needle yelps, grabbing me and Ari by the arms. "Are you all right?"

Everyone's here. The students. The teachers. The three crew members. And Principal Lochner, who makes his way over to us.

"Where are we?" Ari asks. "What's happening?"

"We don't know," Ms. Needle says, talking at a million miles an hour. "We were evacuating the 118, heading down to the hangar bay, when we started hearing that strange countdown. But—just as it ended—these people came out of nowhere. Right out of thin air. We couldn't see their faces. They were wearing armor. Masks. I'm almost glad you weren't there. It was terrifying. They *shot* us. Knocked us out and brought us here!"

"I think the same thing happened to us," I say.

"I'm so sorry," Ms. Needle continues, speaking even faster than before. She's exploding with guilt. "We didn't notice you were gone until it was too late! We were already boarding the shuttles when we took attendance again. I don't know how I lost track of you three. You were *my* responsibility. But we wanted to get everyone off the ship. We were running so quickly. And that voice, it was counting down to—I don't know what. We almost left the ship—left the ship without you . . ."

She trails off, her eyes swimming with tears. Now I'm exploding with guilt too. I mean, there's no reason for her to feel like she abandoned us.

"It's okay," I tell her. "*We* wandered off."

She opens her mouth and leaves it open. Principal Lochner crosses his arms. "Where exactly did you go?"

But I can't actually answer that question, right? *Play it cool, Jack. Just play it cool.*

"Um, we were in the bathroom?"

Ms. Needle raises her eyebrows so high, they look like they might fly off her forehead.

"He means," Becka clarifies, "that I left my mother's necklace—you know, Ms. Needle—the one she gave me for my tenth birthday. It was my great-grandma's. Family heirloom." She's clutching a silver chain around her neck like it's the most precious thing in the world. "I left it in my backpack outside the bathroom near the dorms. And I didn't want to go alone. Didn't think that was smart, you know? So Jack and Ari volunteered to come along. I'm so sorry. We were just gone for, like, two minutes. We should have told you first. But things were so crazy. I just wasn't thinking straight. All I knew was that I couldn't lose my Nana Sue's necklace."

Wow. Just—wow.

Principal Lochner glances from me to Becka to Ari and back again. I'm not sure he bought it, but Ms. Needle is nodding like Becka's story makes perfect sense and is the most beautiful thing she's ever heard. "Well, I'm just glad we're all together now . . . Oh, Ming! How is your arm?"

She rushes over to check on Ming, who's still holding their arm like it's broken. I whisper to Becka, "Was that necklace really your grandma's?"

She shakes her head. "Nah. Fished it out of the trash in the teachers' lounge."

"Gross."

Becka just grins, which means that she's now either lying to *me* for no reason or proudly wearing someone's garbage jewelry.

But before I can ask any more questions, another opening appears at one end of the hallway.

"Next!" a voice says from all around us. The same voice from a minute ago. No one moves a muscle and it thunders again. "I said, 'next'!"

Principal Lochner takes a deep breath. "You want to know what's happening?" he says to Ari in a low voice. "I think we're about to find out."

He squeezes his way through the crowd to stand protectively at the front of the group, right in front of the opening. I see him adjust his tie and even try to button his jacket. But it won't close and he gives up.

9

Okay, picture a football stadium. Now double the size. Actually, scratch that. Picture a space ten times the size of a football stadium. Replace the seats with a million overlapping pieces of dark glass like the stands are made of mountains of truck-sized black diamonds. Replace the green turf of the playing field with—just go with me here—a bottomless pit. And replace the cheerleaders and the hot dogs and the foam fingers with an uncomfortable tingling on the back of your neck.

Fine, so maybe the nightmare bowl we're now standing at the edge of isn't *exactly* like a football stadium. But I don't know how else to describe it. There *is* a smooth glass dome high above us, stretching over the whole place. Two years ago, over winter break, my mom took me to a game at the new Patriots stadium they built on Mars. This kind of reminds me of that. Except, you know, more terrifying.

Far out ahead of us, sticking up from the center of

the pit, is a giant pillar topped with a flat surface. We're still too far away to see anything clearly. But it looks like there are two people up there, one sitting in a chair behind a desk and the other standing to the side, like a guard on duty.

"Move along," the disembodied voice tells us as we all shuffle in from the hallway. The sound echoes around this giant chamber, bouncing across the pit—back and forth, back and forth—until it dies out. *Move along. Move along. Move along. Move along.*

"What *is* this place?" Becka asks.

I shrug and look over at Ari, his jaw wide open, his eyes huge. I know that look. He's not scared or confused. Ari's *excited*.

"Like, maybe we're on some secret government base or something?" Becka continues. "Or maybe—is this Peru? It could be, I guess. I did okay in Spanish last year."

Ari rolls his eyes. "This is definitely not Peru," he says.

And I don't know whether to give him a high five for talking back to Becka or laugh in his face because of what he's about to say.

"Look around." Ari gazes up at the dome and down into the pit. "None of this is, well, *human*."

I snort. There it is.

Don't get me wrong—I'm usually willing to tolerate Ari's fantasies. But this just doesn't seem like the time. How many years have people lived on Mars now?

Literally *hundreds*? Humans have dug up every inch of that dusty planet—and all the others in our solar system too—without finding any evidence of intelligent life that isn't us. And still, every fall, Ari comes back to school believing in another Martian conspiracy theory. He's a sucker for that kind of stuff. The Martians are invisible. The Martians live in the sewers. The Vice President is a secret Martian. Once, I came back from summer vacation with a really short haircut and Ari quizzed me on "things only the *real* Jack would know."

"What're you saying?" I ask him. "That the lady making announcements over the loudspeaker is an *alien*? That we're on some—some alien planet?"

In the span of two seconds, Ari's face rides an emotional rollercoaster: First, he half-smirks—because, yeah, that's exactly what he thinks. But then he looks over at Becka and wipes the smile off his face—because, you know, maybe she's not totally into his supreme dorkiness. And then he does another 180, crosses his arms, and glares at me.

"Come on," he says. "What else could this place be?"

The voice booms all around us in its bored monotone. Weirdly, it sounds British.

"You have been charged with violating criminal ordinance number 7634, section three, part one, subparagraph eleven. On the record before us, you have been found guilty. Please come forward to pay your fine or receive your sentence." *Sentence. Sentence. Sentence. Sentence.*

A platform materializes in front of Principal Lochner, where the edge of the floor drops off like a cliff. It's wide enough that all of us could easily stand on it, but it's barely a centimeter thick and completely see-through, like a large pane of glass turned on its side.

"Please come forward to pay your fine or receive your sentence," the lady says again. *Sentence. Sentence. Sentence. Sentence.*

In any of our normal lives, we probably wouldn't have stepped onto a paper-thin rectangle floating over a bottomless pit in the center of a rocky diamond canyon because a strange angry voice was telling us to. But nothing about this says "normal lives." So—after Principal Lochner tests it with a tiptoe, and then his full weight—on we step. And as soon as the last of us leaves the ledge behind, the platform begins to inch across the chasm, floating toward the center of the stadium.

Ari is giving me an "I told you so!" stare and Becka is nodding over at Ari with newfound respect. But I still don't buy it. I may not understand what's going on, but aliens? Come on.

"So," Becka says to Ari, with an absolutely straight face, "you think this lady is, like, the alien queen?"

Ari's eyes brighten up. "Yeah," he says. "Yeah, I think so."

Ugh. Maybe she's perfect for him after all.

"But why would the alien queen speak English,

71

Ari?" I ask. "And why would she speak it like *that*? Is the alien queen British?"

"She could be using some kind of translator," Ari says, digging in.

"Shhh," Principal Lochner snaps at us.

And now I notice that the teachers and crew have formed a protective circle all around the kids, Principal Lochner up front. And every five or ten feet, someone else: Mr. Cardegna; Harriet, the ship captain; even Mrs. Watts (although she doesn't look all that enthusiastic about the job). The sight of them makes me feel a little better—until I remember that the biggest problems these adults usually face are broken dorm toilets and plagiarism. I'm not sure they're any match for this place, whatever it is.

The floating platform moves slowly across the canyon and, as we approach, the two people on the center column come into focus. The one in the middle is wearing a long, grey cloak with a hood draped over her face. Snow-white hair falls past her knees. She *is* sitting at a desk, like I thought. Only the "chair" is more like an angled wall that she's leaning against, and the "desk" is just one of those dark diamonds from the edges of the stadium, sawed off and turned on its side. The one standing next to her is armored and masked, holding a gun. Maybe one of the soldiers Ms. Needle saw onboard the 118. Maybe the same one who shot at me, Ari, and Becka. The soldier's outfit is silver plated from head to toe, but splotched with dozens of randomly placed copper circles, like a medieval knight rolled around in glue and ancient pennies.

The platform stops right in front of them, about two feet lower than the top of the column. Immediately, the one sitting down raises her hands. Hands that don't look normal. Don't look *human*. Her skin is milky white. And her fingers are pointy, almost claw-like. She pulls back her hood and—there isn't any question now. My chin drops so far down that it practically hits the bottom of the bottomless pit. Ari was right.

Aliens.

Is it weird that my first thought is *Dad would have loved this*?

Her skin and fingers are the most non-human things about her, aside from her deep red eyes, which don't just look like they're covered by red contact lenses. The eyes are *entirely* red. There's no white part. Just two ovals the color of blood dotting a powder-white alien face. She's terrifying. And also she's chewing gum.

"Okay," she says, smacking her lips and blowing a bubble. Yep. The alien queen is chewing gum. Obviously. "We're just going to need a little preliminary information first. So, where are you all from?"

No response from the crowd. We're too busy *looking at an alien*.

"Well?" she asks, our faces blank and mouths wide open. "Come on. There's a long line behind you and

I'm off the clock in an hour." We crane our necks to glance backward. But there's no one else here. "Don't make this worse for yourselves," she adds. "Where are you from?"

The idea that this could somehow get "worse" is enough to jolt Principal Lochner out of his daze. "Um." He clears his throat. "We're from the PSS 118. A school in orbit around Ganymede."

She blows another bubble. "Is Gannermeep supposed to mean something to me?"

"Ganymede."

"Right," she says impatiently, fidgeting with a bracelet on one of her wrists. "That's what I said. I'm going to need a bit more to go on than that."

"Oh," he says. "Okay. Well, Ganymede is one of Jupiter's moons?"

She taps a bunch of her fingers against the surface of her "desk," as if the giant rock—with no screens, no buttons, no holograms—is some kind of computer.

"No record of it. I need coordinates. Quadrants. Numerical planetary designations. Something."

"Um," Principal Lochner stutters. "I . . . I don't know any of that information. We're near Jupiter? Orbiting at about six million miles, I think."

"The Milky Way," Ari offers.

"The Milky Way," Principal Lochner repeats.

"Milk?" She leans forward and squints at us, confused. "No thank you. I'm not thirsty."

Principal Lochner shakes his head. "Never mind," he tells her. "Earth. We're from Earth."

"Hun," the alien queen says, plucking the chewed-up gum out of her mouth and flicking it into the abyss. "I've never heard of it."

"Of course." Principal Lochner nods. "Sorry. Maybe if we can get back to our ship, I could try to give you some of the information you're looking for."

"Nice try," she says, poking different spots on her rock desk. "Make this more complicated. Fine, I can scan you myself."

A beam of pink light shines down from the glass dome, washing over us. Back and forth. Back and forth.

"That's odd," she says, pressing down again and scanning us for a second time, then a third.

Slowly, something dawns on her.

"Wait. Is this an *awakening*?" she asks, looking up from the rock. Before anyone can figure out how to respond, she shouts, "Of course! An awakening! Can you believe it?"

She poses that last question to the guard standing stiffly to her left, slapping one of the armored legs. Her nails clank against the metal and he sways back and forth like a bowling pin hit by a slow ball.

"He can't believe it," she tells us, lowering her voice to a whisper for a moment. "Lois is a little shy." Lois? "Anyway, there hasn't been an awakening around here in a long time. This is *so* exiting. To be honest, I assumed that the galaxy was entirely awakened by now. Didn't think there was anyone left out there still stuck in their own star systems. I wonder if I'll get a raise." She looks at the guard again. "Do you think I'll get a raise?"

Again, Lois says nothing, but the alien lady doesn't seem to care. "Of course not," she laughs, rolling her eyes (a gesture that's somehow TERRIFYING when she does it). "You're right as always."

She turns back to face us. "Well," she says. "What now? Think, think." She's swiping and smacking and scrolling all over the rock in front of her. "Just elephant with me for a moment."

I think she means "*bear* with me." Which means that Ari's theory about a (less than perfect) translation device is probably right.

"I've never presided over an awakening before. Ceremony, you understand. It's in the manual and all government employees get a short training when we're hired. But no one expects . . . Come on . . . Where is it? Ah, yes! Found it! Okay, okay."

Flattening her robe with her branchy fingers, she stands up straight for the first time. She's at least seven feet tall and towers over the much shorter guard.

"Ahem," she begins, staring down at the "desk" and awkwardly reading from some script. "New arrivals! It has come to my/our—er, no, sorry, just my—it has come to *my* attention that this is the first time members of your species have encountered an alien race. It is a great milestone in your history and you, as representatives of your civilization, will no doubt be remembered for years to come. I/we—ah, no—*I* hereby welcome you, the *insert name of species here* into—er . . . " She looks at Principal Lochner. "Sorry. What are you called?"

In a dazed voice, he says, "Um, Jerry Lochner."

"Good, good." She goes back to reading. "I hereby welcome you, the umjerrylochners, into the galaxy. It is diverse and peaceful, bound together by the League of Independent Systems. This is the Great and Wonderful Elvid System, which is presided over by our Benevolent and Perfect Minister. We trust that you will be productive and respectful members of the larger community." She looks up, like she's waiting for something.

"So . . . are we free to go?" Principal Lochner asks.

"Oh no," she chuckles, looking over at the guard like he's in on the joke. "No special treatment, even for the newly arrived umjerrylochners. Rules are rules. Your ship was found in restricted Elvidian space in violation of Criminal Ordinance Number 7634, section three, part one, sub-paragraph eleven. You tripped the alarm when your ship dropped out of light speed into an area off-limits to civilian vehicles."

Light speed?

Ari, Becka, and I look at each other.

What did we do?

"But how are we supposed to get home?" Principal Lochner asks. A desperate note has crept into his voice.

"Not my responsibility. You are welcome to pay the parking ticket and be on your way."

Principal Lochner scrunches up his face in confusion. "Parking ticket."

"That's right. The sentencing guidelines call for a fine ranging from 75 to 150 Elvidian credits. But given the special circumstances"—she smiles a jagged, toothy smile that makes me wish she'd just frown—"I'm willing to impose the minimum."

"So," Principal Lochner clarifies, "you said that's seventy-five, um, what did you call them?"

She leers down at us. "Do you not have any Elvidian credits?" she asks.

"Well, no. I don't think so. But I'm sure we can get you money. Our kind of money. Or, whatever kind of money you want. If we can just go back to our ship for even a few—"

She leans forward all the way over, staring straight down into Principal Lochner's eyes. "Do you or do you not have an Elvidian currency wallet from which you can immediately deposit seventy-five credits into the ministry account?"

His shoulders droop. He closes his eyes. "No."

She takes a fresh stick of gum out of the folds of her robe.

"Shame. I wish I had time to sort this out. But I

don't. They keep us on a tight schedule here. Quotas and such. You understand. In any event, having refused monetary punishment—"

"We didn't refuse!" Principal Lochner cries. "We just can't! We don't know how!"

She glares down at him and pops the gum into her mouth. "Having *refused* monetary punishment, you are hereby indefinitely sentenced to prison until such time as your penalty can be paid." She blows a giant bubble. "*Next!*"

10

I'll catch you up quick. It's been two days. Two days of garlic sand, our black crystal jail cell (which isn't getting any bigger, by the way), and—worst of all—alien school.

Yeah. You heard me. Alien school.

Because the brilliant minds who run this place realized that most of us are kids and not just tiny umjerrylochners. And kids go to school, I guess, even when they're prisoners.

Somehow, alien school is even more boring than normal school. Guards wake us up at the crack of dawn, separate us, and individually place us inside these tiny orb pods that are even worse for my claustronervousness than our cell. We put on these digital contacts that automatically translate the written Elvidian language for us. And then we have the pleasure of spending endless hours doing impossible math problems, trying to answer interstellar geography questions about places we've never heard of, and all around feeling like total dummies.

Ari loves it.

But there *is* some good news. Toward the end of each session we get a chance to ask questions, and the pod computers answer them (sort of). Here are some of mine from Day One:

Question: "What planet are we on?"

Answer: "Elvid IV. Long live the Minister."

Question: "Who's the Minister?"

Answer: "She is the Benevolent and Perfect Minister. Long live the Minister." (Super informative.)

Question: "How can you speak English?"

Answer: "All Elvidians wear translator bracelets that automatically blah blah blah." (I tuned out there.)

Question: "Why do Elvidians have chewing gum?"

Answer: "Chewing gum is the sole invention separately created by every sentient race in the galaxy. Long live the Minister."

Question: "How far away are we from Earth?"

Answer: "Unable to respond."

Question: "Do you know anything about a quarantine?"

Answer: "Unable to respond."

Question: "Are you ever going to let us go?"

Answer: "Unable to respond."

But even if we're not getting straight answers, the school sessions are still an opportunity to gather intelligence. And figure out how we can escape.

By "we," I mean the three of us. We haven't seen

anyone else from the 118 since our sentencing. I assume our classmates have spent the last couple of days in their own pods, and who knows what the adults are up to. But since we have no way of communicating with them, we've decided it's up to us to get out of here, find a way home, and bring back help for the others.

Now we're just back from our second day of alien school, and Ari is pumped. "Today was amazing!" he reports. "The pod taught me a whole new kind of math. And I think I might be able to terraform my backyard when we get home. And—"

I interrupt Ari's speech. "Speaking of getting home, what did you find out in your pod today, Becka?"

She's leaning against a corner, tossing our empty water bucket up and down. "Nothing," she answers.

"Helpful," I say.

She just glares at me, which I try not to take personally. We're all trapped and scared and restless—not to mention hungry. (In a few minutes, a guard will be in with more water and garlic dirt, which is literally the *only* thing they give us to eat.) Becka spent most of yesterday insisting that she's not leaving this system without Diana. We've convinced her that a full-scale jailbreak isn't something we can pull off, but now she's in a foul mood.

"What?" she says back, lying down and staring up at the black ceiling. "What could I possibly ask that would help us get out of here? The stupid school pods are never going to answer any real questions. They're never going to let us go. I'm never going to see my parents again. I might never even see Diana again. And she's probably just down the hall."

I shake my head. "You're wrong," I say. "*I* learned something useful today. The pod had a system update, I think. With new information from scans of the 118. It told me that we're four hundred light years away from Earth. And that our ship got here with a newly built light speed engine."

Becka laughs—a cold, angry laugh. "Oh, how useful!" she says sarcastically. "We're only *four hundred light years* away from home, huh? That's great. Good thing it wasn't *five* hundred or we'd have *no hope* of getting back."

"But the ship has a light speed engine," Ari whispers. "Awesome. Einstein, Shmeinstein. Your *dad* is the greatest physicist of all time."

So okay, my dad apparently built a light speed engine, in secret, in facilities that were far from state-of-the-art. And okay, that makes him the first human to figure out how to travel fast enough to move around the galaxy. But—unless I'm even worse at history than I thought—I'm pretty sure Einstein never accidentally got a bunch of kids arrested by aliens.

And no matter how "awesome" Ari thinks this is, I would have preferred a different version of the story: Once upon a time, Allentown Graham invented some cool technology and sold it to the government or a multiplanetary corporation or something and he got super rich and bought a tropical island on Earth and then all of us—my dad, my mom, and me—chilled in hammocks and drank out of coconuts with twirly straws and lived happily ever after.

"It's perfect!" Ari whoops. "The light speed engine can get us home! All we have to do is get back to the 118, fly to Ganymede, tell everyone there what happened, and come back here with help for the others."

"Suuuuure," says Becka, rolling her eyes. "Simple. Except we can't actually get back to the 118. We don't even know where the 118 *is*."

Ari breaks into a grin. "Actually," he says, "that's the other thing learned today."

Becka slowly sits up, listening.

"What do you mean?" I ask.

He shrugs. "I asked the pod to show me a map of this building and the surrounding area. I know where the ship is.

"Why wasn't that literally the first thing you said after we got back here?" Becka asks, shooting to her feet.

Ari shrugs again, and tilts his head at her. "Because I thought you'd think the terraforming thing was cool?"

"Unbelievable." She shakes her head at him. Ari looks back at her, disappointed.

"So where's the ship?!" Becka demands.

"Shhh," Ari hisses. "What if there's a guard in the hallway?" He lowers his voice again. "What if they're listening to us *right now*?"

"Well," she says, yelling up at the ceiling, "then it's too late! We've misbehaved! Broken the rules! Suspend us from school, please! Expel us!"

Ari shushes her again. "The ship is on the roof of this building," he whispers. "Down the hallway and up."

Becka beams. "Awesome! I was afraid we'd have to trek to the other side of the planet or something."

"I wouldn't say it's awesome," Ari cautions. "That map was pretty intense. Even if we manage to get out of the cell, we'll still have to get past guard stations and laser alarms and secure access points and cameras. I have no idea how we can possibly sneak out of here without being caught."

I slouch down, deflated. We're so far out of our league. The three of us against the galaxy? It's hopeless.

The guard walks in with his daily garlic and water delivery. He's wearing the same metal armor as the silent guard from the stadium—just with fewer pennies glued to his chest. He grunts at us like *he's* annoyed that we're in here and drops the two buckets. Then he steps back out, closing the doorway behind him. We wait a few seconds before resuming our conversation.

"If only we could communicate with everyone else," I say as Ari scoops up some powder for his dinner.

"Whoa," he says, because I guess he likes the stuff even *more* today than usual.

"If only we had a weapon," Becka chimes in.

"If only—" I pause when I hear a click.

The little cell lights up with the same two flashlight stickers Ari made when this all started.

"Your *Pencil*?" Becka asks, awestruck.

Ari nods, holding the little nanoprinter up over his head, like a videogame character who just fished a jewel out of a treasure box.

"It was buried in the garlic," he says. "*Magic* garlic." He closes his eyes tight like he's making a wish. Then he opens them again and rakes the sand pile with his fingers, as if there might be more to find. (There isn't.) I can't imagine how the Pencil found its way into our rations, but I'm guessing magic wasn't involved.

Becka plucks both light stickers out of the air and turns them over and over in her hands like she's doing a card trick. Her grim expression fades, replaced by the trademark mischievous glint in her eyes.

"I think," she says, "we've just found our way out of here."

11

"You ready?" Becka asks Ari.

"Almost," he says, wiping the sweat from his forehead. He's busy writing out his thousandth line of computer code. He's been at it so long that his finger-bunches might fall off. "I want them to be realistic."

"Just do the best you can," she says.

I cross my arms. "For the record," I say, "I still think this is a bad plan. A bad, stupid, bad plan."

"Not like you've come up with anything better."

She has a point. Last night I shot down about a dozen other ideas before we landed on this one. This is the best of the worst ideas, but that doesn't mean I have to feel optimistic about it. "I just don't think anyone will fall for it."

"If we were back home," Becka replies, "this definitely wouldn't work. But we're not back home. The Elvidians don't know anything about us. So how are they supposed to know when we're lying and when we're not?"

I still don't totally buy it. But I appreciate that she's making an effort to convince me. I've seen how arguments with Becka usually play out. She tends to bulldoze her way forward without caring what other people think.

I open my mouth to list all the ways the Elvidians could definitely know we're lying, but Ari announces—

"I'm done."

So I keep quiet. Trying + failing to escape > not trying.

Right?

"Let's get started," Becka says.

Ari takes a long breath, clicks twice, and dispenses what he's been designing with his Pencil: Blisters. Or bad zits. Or nasty bug bites. Whatever they are, he made them look really icky. There are tiny bead ones, long scar ones, thick lumpy ones. Plastic stickers, basically. But *very* realistic plastic stickers. Hundreds of them, floating in front of our eyes.

"Ewwwww," Becka says with admiration.

"Gross," I agree, touching one of the stickers. It plops to the ground, oozing a bit as it hits the floor.

Ari's beaming. "You think they're good?"

"They're awesome," Becka assures him. "And they're gonna be really useful when school—human school, I mean—starts back up again."

I almost say, "You're so sure this is going to work that you're already planning for next year?" But I decide to let it go. Maybe sometimes her overconfidence is a good thing. Maybe.

"Shall we?" Ari asks.

And the three of us put the stickers on our skin one by one. On our faces, our necks, our arms, and our hands.

"You look . . . sick," I say, once we're done. And they do. Like they have the measles or something. On purpose, Becka pops a fake boil here and there on her cheeks and along her left arm, making her look like she has a particularly bad strain of whatever we've come down with. And we wait until the wall opens and our guard walks in. Like we rehearsed, we slump down to the floor and worm around in pretend pain.

"What's happening in here?" he asks.

When the three of us were deciding on our escape plan, Becka wanted Ari to make a gun with his Pencil and shoot the guard when he walked in. I protested that we shouldn't hurt anyone, so she suggested a stun gun. But what good would that do? There are still all the other guards and cameras and locked doors between here and the ship.

Becka's Plan C involved us making a fake gun. (Noticing a pattern here?) Threaten the guard. Tell him that we'd shoot "or else!" Then use him as a hostage to wind our way up toward the top level. But I vetoed that plan too. What if the other guards in the corridor don't *care* that we've taken a hostage? What if it just makes them madder? More likely to use their own giant weapons?

Instead, here we are, covered in fake rashes, squirming around on the cold ground. Not my idea of a great plan either. But at least the risk of sparking a shootout is relatively low.

"We . . ." Becka croaks, "we're siiiiiicccckkkk."

I've got to admit it: Becka sounds great. Her sick voice is *very* believable.

"Soooo ssssiiiiiiicccccck," Ari bellows.

Um. Yeah.

If we were in human school, any teacher would see right through him. But all he needs to do is fool an alien, right?

"Cough, cough," Ari says, as if he's reading the words from a book. "Sneeze, sneeze."

Ugh.

"What's wrong?" the guard asks, putting down the food and water. He steps a foot closer to us and I shout: "No! Stay back."

He listens.

"We have—"

Uh oh. We made all these plans. Ran through every possible scenario. But we never came up with a *name* for our fake disease. I glance over at Becka, who's got "Don't look at *me*!" eyes, then over at Ari, who just says:

"Cough sneeze?"

Think, Jack. Come on! You know the name of at least one disease. Your mom is a doctor! "We have the . . . cold?"

Becka snorts and almost cracks up—but spins her fit of laughing into a fit of coughing.

"The Colllllld," she repeats, drawing the word out like she's telling a ghost story. "It's the worst disease there is. Super contagious."

"Even aliens can catch it!" Ari screams.

The guard steps back. "I . . ." he stutters, "I'll get a doctor."

"No!" we all yell.

"You're already infected," I explain. "It's airborne. We have medicine—a cure—on our ship. We need to get to it right away."

He looks down at me through his shiny black helmet. His face is covered—not that I'm great at reading Elvidian expressions anyway—but I know a skeptical head tilt when I see one.

"And how can you possibly know that I've been infected?" he asks.

This is where we really have to sell it. I remind myself that this guy doesn't know anything about humans and that he can't afford to take any chances. Who knows what the umjerrylochners are capable of?

"Didn't you hear her?" Ari responds without missing a beat. "*Super. Contagious.* Like, if we were home, they'd already have quarantined us."

I nod at him. Good callback.

"And tell me," Becka adds, "how are you feeling?"

"Fine," the guard says.

"Are you sure?" she asks. "You're not"—she shivers for effect—"cold?"

He shuffles his clanky armor feet. "I—maybe? Maybe a little."

Becka glances over at Ari, concerned.

"It's begun," she says, shaking her head. "He'll be frozen solid in hours."

Ari nods. "He'll make a beautiful ice sculpture." The two of them are playing pretty well off each other. Not that I'd ever tell Ari that.

"Enough!" the guard shouts. "Where is this medicine?" He lifts his wrist up to his helmet. His translator bracelet doubles as a communicator, I guess. "Tell me and I'll call one of my superiors so that it can be brought here at once. And the Minister must be informed immediately."

"No!" I yell again. The Elvidians are obsessed with the Minister, if you haven't noticed. "You can't call anyone."

This is it. The icing on top of our lie cake. We figured the guard would try to call for backup. But we need *him* to take us to the ship. Alone.

"The disease," I explain, pretending it's hard for me to sit up. "The Cold. It's so contagious that you can even catch it through computers!"

"You mean . . ." the guard says, sounding horrified,

"that if I word to someone through my comm . . . the person on the other end could catch the disease?"

"No," Becka tells him. "If you word to someone, they *will* catch it. And soon this whole planet will be infected."

"I mean," Ari chimes in, "if you don't think that the Minister will mind getting sick and dying a super painful death and absolutely knowing that it was your fault, then go ahead. Give her a cough—er, a call. But if not, we should go get the medicine ourselves before anyone else gets sick. And we need to hurry!"

The guard stares at us, silent for ten seconds. Twenty.

"Get to your floor walkers," he finally says, swiveling his helmet to look at all three of us in turn and nudging his gun into our chests. "We will go. But I swear on the life of the Minister that if this is some kind of trick, you will quickly learn that there are much, much worse things in this universe than going to school."

12

I can't believe this is working.

The guard leads us out of our cell and down the corridor. As we reach the end of the hallway—the one opposite the gigantic courtroom chamber—we see rooms to his right and left: guard stations, each with a dozen armored soldiers looking at holograms and screens. They immediately stop what they're doing and silently stare in our direction. A few draw their weapons.

"We're fine here," our guard says, stepping forward and waving his wrist-cuff in front of some invisible scanner. I was definitely right about not coming up here guns blazing. Wouldn't have gone well.

The wall in front of us dissolves and we step into a small, boxy chamber. Ari mouths a word to me: "Elevator."

I nod as the opening closes behind us and we shoot up toward the roof of the building. This guard doesn't trust us. He keeps his gun jabbed into one of our backs at all times. But so far, so good.

The elevator comes to a sudden stop and opens up onto the roof. Thanks to the school pods, I know that Elvid IV's atmosphere is breathable, but I'm still nervous as I step forward. I've *never* been outside on the surface of a planet, directly underneath a sun. On Ganymede, most of the public spaces are covered by large domes that keep in the recycled air. Sometimes, if you squint, you can make out the pinprick sun through the glass, far off in the distance. They also pump in UV light during the day to keep us from going bonkers. But it's not the same.

There's only one place in our solar system where you can breathe real air and feel real sunshine. And you can't grow up in space—breathing stale oxygen and looking at pictures of kids playing football on real, grows-from-the-actual-ground grass—without dreaming of one day going to Earth.

Most families in the outer colonies spend years saving up for one trip. My parents always hinted that we'd go sometime before I started high school—though they stopped dropping those hints as soon as they got divorced. When my mom took her new job in California, not only did she not invite me to live with her, she didn't even ask if I wanted to come out for the summer. And once my dad was fired, our finances were even tighter than usual, so a round-trip Ganymede/Earth flight wasn't in our budget.

In the end, it was probably for the best. I'm not sure "alien abduction" is a valid excuse for getting tickets refunded.

My eyes adjust to the light and I look up at the two—is that three?—suns rising in the reddish/orange sky above Elvid IV. Closing my eyes for a moment, I feel the heat against my cheeks. It's not California, but it'll do. I exhale and open my eyes to get a better look at—hello!—the first alien planet humans have ever visited.

We're close to the edge of the roof, standing on the flat top of a black skyscraper. Actually it's more like a huge glass rock sticking up and out of the planet's surface a hundred stories into the air. It doesn't look human-made (or, Elvidian-made, I guess). It looks like it's been here forever. Like the alien construction workers carved rooms out of an already existing pillar.

"Whoa," Ari says.

Yeah. Whoa.

We're *really* high up and can see for miles. Jagged black crystals—like the one we're standing on—blanket the horizon, twisting in and around themselves, criss-crossing at weird angles. It's hard to describe: A million black, overlapping Washington Monuments? A forest of dark glass? Something like that.

"The planet looks like a giant sea urchin," Ari says.

Or that.

It's not like *everything's* a crystal: There are landing pads and tarmacs dotting lots of flat-topped skyscrapers like ours. And, leaning over the edge, I can see the stadium at the foot of this building. But yeah, mostly, Ari nailed it: giant sea urchin.

I look up again into the sky, which is starting to turn a dark shade of blue. Four moons—which remind me of home and make me a little sick for a second—dot the space between the three suns. There are a few ships flying around in the distance. But there isn't much going on up here, above the surface. It's a lot emptier and quieter than I would have thought.

"We aren't sightseeing," the guard says, pushing his gun into Ari's back.

"Right," Ari agrees. "Cough."

There are eight or nine ships parked on this platform, each one weirder than the next. To the left of the 118 is a ship that looks like a sideways letter H, with a hull painted the colors of snakeskin. The body of the ship is so thin, it seems impossible that anyone or anything could actually fit inside *except* a snake. And to the right of the 118 is a smaller ship that looks like a smooth, purple egg with one giant jet engine sticking out the back.

I've never seen the PSS 118 on the ground before, only from a shuttle. From this perspective I barely recognize it. It's bigger than I thought it was, for one thing. It's also even junkier than I realized. The hull has been banged up by years of encounters with stray meteoroids and space parts—not to mention whatever attacked us before we got here. Crewmembers Tim and Georgia (known among the teachers as "not the brightest stars in the galaxy") are constantly taking space walks to repair the hull, which probably accounts for all the misshapen panels with the wrong color paint and screws that haven't been screwed in all the way.

I smile. I've kind of missed our terrible ship.

"How do we get inside?" the guard asks, even though we're standing right in front of the main entrance—the door with a sign that says *Main Entrance.*

Okay, so thanks to the contacts they gave us, I can read the Elvidian language, but this guy can't read mine. Which might come in handy.

"This way," I say, trying to walk with a fake limp. With all the distractions, I have to remind myself to be sick. I look at Ari, who's totally forgotten. He's practically skipping. Becka, on the other hand—'cause she's a total pro—has continued to play it up. She's shivering and chattering her teeth, and can't seem to stop scratching herself. She's popped at least half the stickers on her skin.

I step over to the control panel next to the main door and press my hand to the screen. Students aren't supposed to have this kind of access to the ship, but thanks to my dad, the panel lights up for me right away. Unfortunately, access to the ship means access to the *ship.*

"*WELCOME, JACKSONVILLE GRAHAM,*" it says. Followed by: "*HOLD ON. WHAT IN THE—*"

"Ship," I say, mustering all the confidence I've got. It needs to understand that now's not the time for shenanigans. "Please open this door. And I'm going to need you to stay absolutely quiet, for our guest here. It's the Cold. You understand. Too much noise causes, um, headaches."

It says nothing back: Probably a first. But it's also not opening the door.

"Open," I say again. "Please."

Still nothing. I stare at the panel, wondering how to convince it to trust us. It's got to know we're not in our own solar system anymore. That something's happened. Something that needs to unhappen.

I get an idea and subtly touch a finger to the screen, hoping that the guard's inability to read the sign at the entrance means what I think it means. I write, "911."

And instantly, the door slides open and a ramp unravels at our feet.

For the second time in two minutes, I exhale a long breath.

The hatch leads straight into the hangar bay. As we walk in, the overhead lights turn on—*thunk thunk thunk*, front to back—illuminating the five shuttles parked tightly inside.

"Where's the medicine?" the guard asks. "Quickly."

"This way," I lead, squeezing past some metal storage containers. "There's a hatch that accesses the main corridor." We're only going to have one shot at this. The moment he suspects we're lying to him is the moment our plan ends. Good thing the guard can't read English, since on our quest to get the "medicine," we pass right by a door that says *Infirmary/Nurse's Office*.

Because we're on our way back to the cafeteria instead.

It's just as we left it, with furniture and food scattered everywhere. I have to sidestep a heap of mashed potatoes to reach the control panel.

"We keep the medicine locked in here," I lie, stepping away from the group and putting my hand against the screen. I don't get shot right away, so that's something. And the panel lights up and shows me the display—but the ship stays quiet, just like I'd asked.

"I need to find the right screen," I say, glancing behind me. The guard is pointing his gun right at my back, waiting for an excuse to pull the trigger.

And I'm about to give him one.

"Hurry up," he says.

We talked about the hidden cameras in the cafeteria, right? They're all over the place, watching us from every corner, so small that they're invisible to the naked eye. But it isn't the cameras I need. It's what the cameras are looking at.

Following Becka's instructions—which were frighteningly specific—I finish rerouting the feed *of* the room back *into* the room, streaming the images into the digital paper lining the walls, floor, and ceiling.

"I've got it," I announce, pressing one last button and spinning around.

As planned, the screens around the room begin displaying the room itself, projecting images of us back out again. The cameras pick up what's inside the cafeteria and the walls display what the cameras pick up, which turns our surroundings into a 3D funhouse-version of what happens when you stand between two mirrors. So instead of just Ari, Becka, me, and the guard, there are a whole bunch of Aris, Beckas, mes, and guards scattered around the room.

I look left and, because the cameras are recording me from different angles, some of the images and projections of me look left too, while others look right or up or down. It's dizzying. Even though I'm trying to focus on the *real* Ari, Becka, and guard, I'm having trouble telling the people apart from the holograms.

But the guard isn't having the same problem. I watch as all the versions of him—real and fake—calmly press down onto their silver wrist cuffs.

"I thought you might try something foolish," he says, training his huge gun right at (the real) me. "But I assumed it wouldn't be *this* foolish. Do you really think that my helmet is all for show?"

He taps the side of his head. "Heat vision," he explains. "Your little display is absolutely useless. I know *exactly* where you are."

I hear him charge up his gun.

"And I warned you that if this was a trick, you would regret it."

A shot rings out and a body slumps to the floor.

But it isn't *my* body.

The projections? The holograms? They were all a distraction to get the guard to look away from Ari and Becka long enough for Ari to make one more thing with his Pencil.

See, when I first switched on the projections, the guard focused his attention on me. Ari took out his Pencil and double-clicked, and then Becka grabbed the small item created by the last of the preprogrammed nanorobots in Ari's Pencil and fired one shot.

Like I said: When we came up with this plan, I told Becka no guns. At least, no guns *right away*.

"Bull's-eye," she says, blowing at the barrel of her tiny stun pistol like she just won a duel in an old Western.

I shut off the wallpaper, and Ari triple-clicks his Pencil. The nanorobot pimples on our skin dissolve and so does Becka's stun gun. Dismayed, she turns toward Ari and opens up her empty hand.

"It might be a good idea for me to have a weapon on me all the time. For protection."

But I shake my head. "Let's think about that one later," I say.

She grumbles but lets it go. No time to waste.

The three of us—well, okay, mostly Becka—drag the unconscious guard out of the cafeteria, down the hallway, and into Principal Lochner's office. He's the only faculty member whose office has a chair bolted down to the floor. We heave the guard into it. Ari grabs a bunch of duct tape from the supply closet in the hangar bay and straps him down, using almost an entire roll for each arm and leg.

"I don't think he's going anywhere," Becka says.

Ari steps back to assess the job. "Can't be too careful."

We have no idea how long we've got before someone comes looking for us. If we weren't, you know, prisoners on a hostile alien planet, maybe we'd just try to take off now and hope for the best. But even if the sky *looks* empty, there's no way that it actually *is* empty. If we're going to pull this off, we need a little more information than what Ari was able to get by snooping around inside the school computer.

I look over at Becka, who has that gleam in her eye.

"Now for the fun part," she says, cracking her knuckles.

13

"Tell us!" Becka screams. "Or else!"

This interrogation isn't going as well as I'd hoped. The guard woke up a few minutes ago, right after we removed his helmet. And he was not super pleased to see us.

I look around at all the posters on Principal Lochner's wall—"Settle it with a smile!" "Your moon is where the heart is." "There's no 'I' in Outer Space!"—and wonder whether they might be spoiling the mood.

"You don't frighten me, you puny umjerryloch-ner," the guard growls, his long Elvidian hair whipping around as he tries to free himself. Good thing Ari used all that tape.

"Do your worst," he says, his red eyes getting redder.

The problem is that this *is* kind of our worst. We're not really going to hurt the guy. But Becka's vague threats don't seem to be doing the trick. If she could just challenge him to a one-on-one dodgeball game, he'd be begging for mercy right now. Of course, thanks to me, we don't *have* any more dodgeballs, so that option's off the table.

We only need one more thing from him: To find out what stands in the way of us getting off this planet. Gun turrets? Military ships? Some other planetary defense system? There's gotta be *something*. There's no way we're in the clear yet. Even *if* we can figure out how to get the ship off the ground, we need to know how to get it to safety. But if this guard knows anything that could help us, he's keeping it to himself.

"But we're not just *any* umjerrylochners," Becka informs him. "We're *criminals*. We've done *terrible* things."

"You're in jail for an unpaid parking ticket," he says back.

"Oh sure, sure." Becka nods. "But that's just the latest thing. We've been in and out of jails all over the galaxy. You heard of the Great Asteroid Robbery out in the Tofu System?"

"No."

"Well you should have. That was us. Kidnapping of the troll governor from Planet Barbie? Us. Nuclear Stink Bomb in the Grapefruit Nebula? Us. That was *not* an easy one to pull off, by the way. Barely made it out of there alive. But you can *bet* we got away with Blackbeard's treasure."

Even though she's the best liar in the galaxy, the guard doesn't seem convinced.

"Enough!" he shouts. "Release me at once. The Minister does not take kindly to those who disrespect her soldiers."

Becka rolls her eyes. "Please. The Minister couldn't hit a Snorg with a Blorg if her life depended on it."

Ari chuckles—Becka is now literally talking gibberish—but the guard doesn't seem to find it funny. Those eyes have gone so dark and deep red, they're almost black.

"Did . . . you . . . insult . . . her?"

He's so shocked and angry that he can barely get the words out. He starts thrashing around on the chair so furiously that I'm scared he'll rip the tape clean off his arms. "Minister! Minister! Forgive me!" he screams over and over again, trying to bow down in the chair as far as the duct tape will let him.

Told you they were obsessed.

"Nice work," I say. "You broke him."

"How is this my fault?" Becka asks, as the guard sways back and forth, threatening to pull the chair out of its socket in the floor. "How was I supposed to know he was, like, in love with the Minister?"

The guard immediately stops moving. "Yes. I *do* love the Minister. I *do*."

"Of course you do, buddy," I tell him soothingly. "Of course you do."

This calms him down a little.

"Now," Becka continues, "you might love the Minister, but she can't help you now. Tell us how to get off this planet, tell us if there's anything dangerous out there, and we'll let you go. Simple as that."

"Never," he spits.

I sigh. We're not getting anywhere and the clock is ticking. He might even be stalling on purpose, waiting for his fellow guards to come find him.

"Guys," I say. "Maybe we should just go. Take our chances. We're sitting ducks down here."

Ari nods, but Becka—looking into the alien's face—doesn't seem so sure.

"Yes," says the guard with a sinister grin. Like gum, another thing that's universal: the smile of someone who means you harm. "Don't sit on ducks. Take your chances. Why not?"

I turn to Ari and I think he's changed his mind about leaving. His eyes bulge and his mouth opens wide.

"We'll figure it out," I try to reassure him, but he's looking past me. And now he smiles this big, stupid smile, which I immediately recognize. Because I've seen it pretty recently.

"Oh come on," I say, as Ari bends down underneath Principal Lochner's desk and picks up his hamster.

"Doctor Shrew!" exclaims Becka, who's almost as excited as Ari. "He's okay!"

"Of course he's okay," Ari says. "He's a *doctor.*"

"Can we please focus?" I've just noticed that the tape closest to the guard's long fingernails is shredded and loose. He's still tied down, but who knows how long we can keep him that way.

"Oh yeah." Ari nods. "You're right, you're right."

He turns around to face the guard, holding the doctor (tightly this time) in both hands.

Suddenly—again—the guard's mood changes.

"Arg!" he yells. "What manner of beast is *that*?"

"A hamster!" Ari answers happily. He can talk about Doctor Shrew for hours. Did you know that the human genome is 87 percent hamster? Cause I do. After a *four-hour-long* conversation with Ari.

In a low voice, like he's genuinely afraid, the guard says, "Please—don't let it near me."

Ari looks down into his hands. "Doctor Shrew? He's harml—"

"Ful!" I finish. "He's extremely harmful. He can tear through solid steel with his teeth! Burn through it with his laser eyes!"

"Already?" says the guard. "Even before it reaches its full size?"

"This *is*—" Ari starts to say.

"Only a baby!" I cut him off. "You should see the adult hamsters we have onboard. They're even more ferocious."

Ari and Becka are staring at me as if I've lost my mind.

But I'm staring at the alien—leaning back in Principal Lochner's chair as far as it goes, trying to get away from the tiny animal in Ari's hands.

Doctor Shrew might just save us all.

* * *

Ari and I are in the computer lab, hovering over a microphone and one of the smaller cameras that the A/V club sometimes uses for motion capture. The technical details weren't too complex to figure out. Not with Ari around and with the ship being (mostly) cooperative. The hard part was strapping Doctor Shrew down to the table underneath the camera in a way that satisfied Ari that we weren't "committing animal cruelty."

Becka is over in the cafeteria keeping watch over our prisoner. Against my better judgment, Ari made her another stun gun, and she used it to keep the guard in check while we transferred him from the principal's chair to a rolling desk chair we'd stolen from the nearest classroom. After Ari blew through a fresh roll of duct tape to strap him in, Becka wheeled him off.

Now, I'm watching the cafeteria on one of the screens, and Becka and I are communicating via two small earpiece headsets we also found in the computer lab. She's already duct-taped his chair to one of the lunch tables so that he can't easily wheel himself toward an exit, and she's talked me through rerouting this room's camera feed to one of the cafeteria's walls. Now we're just waiting on Ari. "But I don't know how long this guy's going to behave," she says in my ear.

"Almost there," I tell her, as Ari repositions Doctor Shrew for the tenth time. "Come on, Ari. We need to get started."

"Okay, okay," he says, as he flips a switch and turns on the feed. The wall across from Becka and the guard flickers to life, displaying a fifteen-foot-tall animal, with golden-brown fur and pitch-black eyes staring out from a semi-3D display.

"Nooo!" the guard yells, trying to kick his legs backward to swerve away from the screen. But he's bound to the table and can't get very far. "Begone, foul monster!"

"I think he looks even cuter on the big screen," Becka whispers.

"Let's hope you're wrong," I say back. "Do your thing, Ari."

He gulps, grabs the mic with both hands, and starts speaking in a low, rumbly, epic voice.

"I am *Doctor Shrew*!" he bellows, deep and angry. "Why have you disturbed me?"

"Oh, magnificent doctor," the guard cries, "I am so sorry. I was brought here. Against my will. These children, they—"

"Nonsense!" Ari shouts. Becka turned the volume in the cafeteria up so loud that the room shakes with every word. "These children are my servants! They do my bidding. For I am Doctor Shrew! Demon space hamster of . . . er . . . space!"

The actual, little, Doctor Shrew is wiggling his legs around in tiny makeshift shackles, sniffing around at the carrot I'm dangling in front of him, just out of reach. But he's looking straight enough into the lens of the camera that the hologram in front of the guard peers right at him.

"O great one," the poor guard begs, "please be merciful."

"You displease me!" Ari yells, really getting into a groove. "I am the Rat King! Rodent God of Destruction! Shrew, Lord of—"

I elbow him in the side. "Don't overdo it."

"Sorry," he says away from the mic.

"It's cool," I tell him. "Keep going."

He nods and refocuses. "You have imprisoned my followers on this planet! You must let all of the umjerrylochners go!"

"But I cannot!" the guard says. "I do not have the authority to give such an order, and the Minister would never allow it. I would be punished together with those I set free!"

We figured that one was a long shot. But we had to try. Ari knows to aim lower.

"Fine," Ari says back. "Then at least tell me exactly what awaits this ship if it were to take off. How can we escape this planet?"

The guard hesitates for a second and Ari growls into the mic like a tiger.

"Defy me at your peril," he warns. "I will eat you and everyone on this planet!"

"Please! No! The Minister will be angry!"

"I am angry. You have five seconds," Ari insists. "Five!"

"Please, I can't!"

"Four!"

"You don't understand!"

"Three! Two!"

"Okay! If you let me go—without eating me—I'll tell you how to safely get off Elvid IV."

"Tell me how to safely get off Elvid IV and then I'll let you go without eating you."

The guard slumps down. He seems genuinely scared. If he weren't one of the people keeping us prisoner, maybe I'd even feel bad for him.

"Fine," he says. "It's just a simple code. Broadcast it before you enter low orbit and you should make it past the defenses without incident."

He rattles off a string of numbers.

"Ship?" I ask out loud. "You—"

"*YEAH, YEAH. WAY AHEAD OF YOU. IT'S ALREADY PRIMED TO BROADCAST.*"

"That was amazing," Becka whispers in my ear. "Tell Ari that he's awesome."

I look over at Ari, who's doing a weird victory jig to celebrate his success.

"I think he knows," I whisper back to Becka. But I give Ari a thumbs-up anyway.

"Oh," the guard adds, "and make sure you're out of range of the light speed jammer around the planet. If you use any such engine before passing beyond the enclosure, well, there won't be anything left of your ship when you reach the other side."

Ari freezes mid-jig. "I see," he says into the mic. "Tell me more."

14

"We did it," I say, as we head toward the front of the ship. Once the guard explained how to scan for the light speed jammer, Becka stunned him one more time and we left him outside on the prison roof. Now we're ready to go.

"Shhh!" Ari snaps. "Don't say that!"

"Why?" I ask. "We have the ship. We know how to get us off the planet. And we have my dad's engine to get us home. What could go wrong?"

Ari shakes his head like I've just doomed us all.

"Are you *trying* to jinx us?"

But I'm feeling optimistic for the first time in days. We're almost to the command bridge now. We'll get off this terrible planet. Fly to a distance beyond the range of the jammer, where we can safely use my dad's engine. Go home. Tell everyone what's happened. And bring back help.

Of course, we still don't know what happened with that quarantine. Something attacked us near Jupiter and started counting down. And my dad was so scared of it, he had us run away farther than anyone's ever run before. Whether he was right to be scared or not, I don't know. But I can't wait to make it back to Ganymede and finally get some answers.

First, though, gotta get the ship in the air.

"Whew!" I grunt, as the door to the command bridge slides open and I'm hit with a whiff of old hamburger.

Becka pinches her nose. Ari plucks a plastic plate— with its now greenish meat and stale french fries—off of one of the computer consoles and tosses it down the trash chute. The crew obviously left in a hurry.

I've been here a few times on our "field trips" and the bridge never fails to disappoint me. Wall-to-wall purple shag carpeting that's spotted with more than a few coffee stains. A ceiling that's painted three different shades of yellow, like they ran out of paint in the middle of the job and don't care that it looks like the ceiling of a mustard factory had a terrible accident. And a sign hanging next to the door: "No eating. No loud music. IDs must be worn at all times." Judging by the spoiled lunch, I'm betting Harriet doesn't strictly enforce these rules.

Size-wise, the oval-shaped bridge is pretty small— no bigger than my living room on Ganymede. Along the length of the front wall, there's a large window that doubles as a viewscreen. There's a freestanding captain's chair in the center of the room, facing the window. And behind the chair there are two small computer stations, also facing front. The consoles are bulky and old. Even the captain's chair looks like it's from the twenty-second century. It's covered in loose, scratched-up white leather and, while the armrests each have small access panels at the edges, the one on the left is cracked and clearly broken.

So, yeah, a perfect command bridge for the PSS 118.

"Ari," I ask, "think you can figure this out?"

"Think so."

Ari sprints over to one of the two computer consoles behind the captain's chair. We've all had basic flight lessons, but he's got the most experience. And by "the most experience," I mean "holds the high score in Neptune Attacks 2," our favorite first-person spaceshooter. Well, *my* favorite first-person spaceshooter. Ari thinks the first Neptune Attacks was better. But both games have realistic flight simulators.

"I'm locked out," he says. "It won't let me access flight controls."

"Oh yeah." I press my hand to the flight station. "I forgot. Let me try."

"*WELCOME, JACKSONVILLE GRAHAM.*"

"Hey, Ship. Can *I* use the flight controls?"

"*I DON'T KNOW,*" the ship says back. "*CAN YOU?*"

"That's never a funny joke," I tell it. "You know that, right?"

The ship replies, "*YOU'RE NOT SUPPOSED TO BE HERE. YOU KNOW THAT, RIGHT?*"

"I do, Ship. But those aliens could find us any second. Now do I have access to flight controls or not?"

"*WELL, YOU DON'T HAVE TO GET UPPITY ABOUT IT,*" the ship says. "*AND YES, YOU HAVE ACCESS. I HAVE NO IDEA WHY OR HOW. BUT YOU DO.*"

"Great," I reply. But I can't manage the whole ship by myself. I wouldn't know how if I wanted to. "And what if—? Can I grant access to Arizona Bowman?"

"*AFFIRMATIVE. ALL SYSTEMS TRANSFERABLE EXCEPT LIGHT SPEED CAPABILITIES.*" A pause. "*WAIT. DID I JUST SAY LIGHT SPEED CAPABILITIES?*"

"We'll explain on the way," I tell it, kind of glad that Ari won't get to use my dad's engine. I can't help but want to keep that to myself. I can't explain why, but I do. "For now, give Ari flight controls."

"*ACCESS GRANTED.*"

Ari and I look at each other.

"Well? What're you waiting for?"

Ari smiles huge and starts clicking away at the screen. He presses down on one switch and pulls back on another. I feel the ship rumble beneath my feet and look out the window to see us rising—unevenly at first, but slowly leveling off—up into the air. One foot. Two feet.

"Wahoo!" Ari yells, like he's riding a bull and not gently lifting a hulking ship *one inch at a time, very carefully* up into the sky.

But quickly, things pick up. Ari grows into his "wahoo." Within seconds, we're high above the crystal skyline, speeding toward the upper atmosphere.

Becka's been pretty quiet this whole time, staring at the tacky chair in the middle of the room. But now she says, "Give me access too. I can scan for the light speed jammer and other ships while Ari's doing the piloting."

I hesitate. Having Ari as co-pilot is one thing. Giving Becka access is something else entirely.

"Come on," she says. "Someone needs to monitor how far we've gone so we'll know when it's safe to go to light speed. And it wouldn't hurt to have a heads up if an Elvidian ship is coming our way and decides to shoot at us. Ari's doing the flying, you're doing, um, the light speed stuff, and I should do scanning and comms. Like a real crew."

I've been trying not to think about what'll happen if anything decides to shoot at us. The 118 has no weapons. Like most public schoolships, it was a commercial freighter in its past life. We'll be sitting ducks in a fight, no matter what. But I guess it can't hurt to have someone looking out for danger.

"You heard her," I say to the ship. "Give Beckenham Pierce computer access also."

"*DO I HAVE TO?*"

"What? Yes, you have to."

"*FINE. ACCESS GRANTED. BUT I'M NOT HAPPY ABOUT IT.*"

Becka hustles over to the other console and starts fiddling with her control panel. The ship starts broadcasting the code we got from the Elvidian guard. A minute goes by, and nothing attacks us. Nothing even approaches. Instead, the dark blue sky gives way to starry space and I can see the entire Elvid system stretched out in front of us, all the way down to the three stars in the center.

"How far can autopilot take us?" I ask Ari as he leans back into his chair.

"Not far," he says, pointing to the screen. "There's a counter here. When it's up, I'll have to take direct control."

"How long do we have?"

"A few minutes, maybe."

"Will we be far enough away from the planet to use the light speed engine?"

"Just about," says Becka, looking at a display on her screen.

I nod and lean against Ari's station.

"Did you figure out what you wanted to change the call sign to?"

Every ship, including ours, has a call sign—a signal that broadcasts out to all other ships and tells them who we are. But now, we're fugitives on the run from the alien police. And flying inside a chunk of metal that's screaming, "We are the PSS 118! We are the PSS 118!" might not be the best way to stay under the radar. So when we decided that Ari would be the pilot, we gave him the job of choosing what to call the ship. If he's got to fly it, he may as well name it.

"I've got just the thing," Ari says, grinning and typing something into his console.

I glance down at the screen.

"No," I tell him, shaking my head. I should have figured. "We are *not* renaming our ship the Millennium Falcon."

"Why not? I thought you said that the only rule was that I couldn't name it the Starship Ari."

"Yeah, but shouldn't we come up with something original?"

Before Ari can pout too much, Becka shoves us both out of the way, types a couple of words on his screen, and asks: "What do you think of this?"

Ari and I look down at the screen and back up at each other in surprise. Who knew she had a sentimental side?

"Okay," I tell her. "The Ganymede it is. That's actually a good name, Becka. I'm—"

"Yeah, yeah, whatever. Who cares? Now that that's over with, we have something more important to talk about."

Uh oh. Is something wrong? Is someone coming for us?

"Who gets the captain's chair?" she asks.

So that's why she's been staring at it.

The idea of an official seating arrangement hadn't even occurred to me. We're not going to be out here for long (I hope). But maybe she's right. Two back computer consoles. One captain's chair up front. Three of us. *Someone* should play captain, right?

I watch as Becka steps over to the seat in the center of the room—running her hands over the old leather and staring down at the controls on the arms—and I realize something: now that *she* seems to really want it, so do I.

Before you go thinking that I'm just being a baby, let me clarify that I don't *only* want it because Becka does. I just know that if Becka gets it, she'll confuse *sitting* in the captain's chair with *being* the captain. And I am not taking orders from Captain Becka, even if we're going straight back to Ganymede. But as I look at Becka looking at Ari looking at her, I know that she knows what I know: I don't stand a chance if we put it to a vote.

"So let's put it to a vote." Becka smiles at me. Told you. "That seems like the fair way to figure it out." She pauses for like half a second. "And I vote for me," she adds, raising her hand.

I walk over to the captain's chair and put my hands down on one of the armrests, directly opposite Becka.

"And I vote for *me*," I say, staring her down.

She purses her lips and looks over at Ari.

"And Ari," she asks, "who do *you* vote for?"

"I . . . uh . . . I . . ."

Which is when Ari shocks me.

"Jack," he says, looking down at his shoes and gulping. "Jack should be the captain."

"What?" Becka shrieks. "*Jack?* Why?!"

She storms over to his waist-high computer console, which he is wisely standing behind. But it won't offer him any protection if T-Bex comes out to play. I've seen *Jurassic Moon III*. Dinosaurs in space are *very* dangerous.

"It just makes sense, doesn't it?" Ari explains, circling the console as Becka slowly chases him around it. "Jack's the only one with any real control over the ship, right?" He turns to me. "Without you, I couldn't fly it. Without you, Becka couldn't do, um, whatever it is Becka is going to do. You're the only one who can actually get us home. So you're kind of already the captain, aren't you?"

I hadn't thought of it like that. He's right. I *am* kind of already the captain. Captain Jacksonville Graham.

I don't mind the sound of that at all.

Becka lets out a snort and closes her fists. I watch as her knuckles turn red and expect her to punch a hole in the wall or something. But instead, she shocks me too.

"Fine," she sighs. "Ari's right, I guess. And the vote's the vote." She moves to stand behind the other back computer console.

I really (really!) want to give Becka the credit she deserves for being so calm and reasonable. She wanted to be captain and she's giving it up fair and square. I *definitely* should not rub it in her face. Definitely not.

"You'll have plenty to do," I tell her, taking my seat

in the center of the bridge. "All that scanning, right? And comms! You'll be *great* at that. I'm sure it'll be just as fun as being captain."

"Shut up," she says, gritting her teeth. "You don't have to be a jerk about it."

Well. I *tried* not to rub it in her face. Half-tried.

I swivel around to look at my crew. Ari is staring apologetically at Becka who is giving him the coldest—most freezing—shoulder ever. I stretch my hands out to try to touch the small control pads on the armrests. The chair is actually a little too big for me and I can't reach the consoles without leaning forward. My feet don't even touch the floor.

Becka is taller and probably would've physically fit here better than I do.

But I *belong* here more than she does.

"We're approaching the end of autopilot control," Ari announces as the room lets out a one-second siren. "I think I can fly it myself, if I need to."

"Don't think you'll need to," says Becka. "We're outside the range of the light speed jamming."

"Cool," I say and turn to Ari. "But when we get to the other side, think you can bring us into Ganymede's orbit?"

Ari presses a few buttons and slides a lever back and forth. "Aye, aye, Captain!"

I sit back and grin, interlocking my fingers behind my head.

"Ship," I say, "turn on the light speed engine. Destination: Ganymede."

Like before, the regular engines shut down.

"*ENGAGE?*" the ship asks.

I nod. "Engage," I say, much less conflicted this time around. "Bring us home."

Right on cue, everything goes dark for a second. A fraction of a fraction of a second. Even less time than before. But it works. We move faster than the speed of light, overwhelmed with this strange feeling. We travel in a way that breaks every rule of physics, all because of my dad. Because of him, we move through the fabric of the universe and emerge . . .

. . . um . . .

. . . about thirty or forty feet from where we were before, the three Elvidian suns right where we left them.

"*LIGHT SPEED ENGINE OFFLINE,*" the ship announces. "*FUEL DEPLETED.*"

"What?!" I yell. "Fuel depleted? Ship, why didn't you tell me we were running out?"

"*YOU DIDN'T ASK,*" the ship says.

So we just drift there, staring at the alien solar system, with no way home.

"Yeah," Ari grunts. "*What could go wrong?*"

15

"Well?" Becka chimes in. "What now, *Captain?*"

The ship trembles as the regular engines restart and a few more brutally silent seconds hang in the air. I turn around toward the crew.

"I've got it," Ari says as the 118 tilts to one side. The ship does two groaning summersaults before leveling out.

"*HE'S GETTING IT,*" the ship corrects.

"We're fine," Ari says defensively. "But where am I supposed to go?"

I don't know what to tell him. We're *four hundred light years* away from home. Without a working light speed engine, it'll take us literally forever to get there. I wonder if we made a bad choice. If escaping was a mistake. It seemed like the right thing to do at the time—get away, get help. But now that we're up here all alone, we're no use to anyone.

"Jack?" Becka asks again.

"I'm thinking, I'm thinking."

"No." She shakes her head. "Your ring. Look."

I look down at my hand. She's right. I don't know when it happened. I must've been so distracted that I didn't hear the beep or see it start to glow. But I have a video message. Way out here, an impossible distance away from home. Which means that it can only be from one person.

I open my hand and speak into my palm. "Play the last message," I say. I make a throwing gesture with my hand, which tosses the message to the big window screen in front of us. Our view of space disappears—replaced by the face of my dad, sitting on the couch in our living room on Ganymede.

"Hey Jack," he says into the camera. "This is a recording. Obviously. And if you're watching this, well, I've probably made a huge mistake."

He's wearing a pair of jeans and a plaid, button-down shirt. He looks like he always looks: silly, smart, and itching to get up and run in circles. His right leg is shaking up and down like he drank too much coffee. I don't know when he created this message. But I don't think it was after the attack.

"I saved this video to your ring," he continues, "and hid it in an invisible file folder. It's only supposed to play if I don't reset a remote clock on my end every few days. So if you're able to access the recording, something's happened to you, or me, or both. And I think I know why. Well, sort of."

I take a deep breath and turn around for a second to look at Ari. His eyes are wide. He knows that I've been waiting months for some kind of explanation. It's only a recording, I know. But it's something.

"Let me start at the beginning," my dad says. "I've always performed my own personal experiments in my free time. You know that. Played around with inventions and ideas."

He leans forward and puts his hands on his knees like he does when he's excited about something. "Then, at the beginning of this school year—around August or September—I figured something out. I was mixing and matching formulas for a chemical compound that was supposed to power the apartment at half the cost. Instead I ended up creating a workable Alcubierre drive that could be interwoven with almost any ship's thrusters . . ." He waves his hand. "The science doesn't matter. The point is, Jack, I did it. Solved a riddle that's been in humanity's way for centuries: How to travel at the speed of light. How to travel *faster*. Much faster."

He sits back again, like the thrill of it still blows him away.

"It was incredible. I don't know how much of the credit I can take. It was kind of an accident. But it was *my* accident."

"I wanted to tell you right away. Tell your mother. Tell *everyone*. And then, something strange happened. I was on my computer in the science lab—I hadn't actually built anything yet. I was just using the theoretical compiler and a few Pencils to mock up the design. And within seconds of putting the fuel molecule together—quantum hexachloride—I got a message. I don't know who it was from. I tried to trace the source every way I know how, but never could. Whoever it was worked hard to cover their tracks."

My dad pauses. His voice is lower when he continues, like this next part is serious. Dangerous.

"That first message was only a single word: 'No.' But they kept coming: 'Stop this.' 'It will bring only trouble.' Things like that, longer and longer every time. Then, a couple of weeks later, just as I was getting ready to begin the real work of building the engine, I received the last message. It was longer than the others. More personal. Every single word stuck in my brain. It said, 'These are not threats. They are warnings. If what you are creating is detected, it will bring destruction upon all those you care about. Turn back, before it is too late.'"

My dad smirks.

"Heavy, right? It seemed unbelievable to me. Still does. Maybe it's some hacker who's playing a practical joke. Or a mega-corporation, trying to prevent this technology from disrupting the propulsion industry. I don't know. But I wasn't going to let it stop me—not when I was on the verge of something important. Something that would allow humankind to explore the universe. It's bigger than me. Bigger than all of us."

I hear the words he's saying and, in my brain, I know that he's right. He *needed* to finish his work. It was too important to stop. But my emotions are all mixed up. He *knew* that something bad could happen? He put me in danger *on purpose*? Light speed or not, shouldn't *I* be the most important thing in his life?

"Still," my dad continues, like he's reading my thoughts, "if there was even a chance that going public with what I was doing would put you at risk, I couldn't take it. Believe me, hitching humanity's first light speed engine to the PSS 118 wasn't my first choice. But I didn't see any other safe way to continue my work without a ton of red tape. And I kept it all a secret. From you, from your mother, from Principal Lochner, from the ship's crew. I mean, I knew someone on the 118 would realize something was up eventually. I'd get spotted going into or leaving the engine room at the very least. So I made a hundred other pointless modifications to throw everyone off track in case I was found out. And hid the real work—the heart of what I was building—inside a small, secret panel deep within the engine room. Only you and I can access the panel and only you and I can trigger the software that runs the relevant program."

He shrugs and grins at me again.

"And everything pretty much worked out. By the time I got busted for unauthorized use of the engine room, the job was done. I was only running a few last-minute diagnostic tests. And I have to admit it was a little amusing to see everyone freak out over those use-less decoy wires I added to the fusion reactor."

I hear Ari speak from behind me.

"So this video is from *after* he got fired?"

I nod. "I guess so."

"I'm sorry for that day, Jackie," my dad says. "I know how rough it was for you and how angry you were at me. You haven't really taken my calls lately, and I get it. I've kept tabs on you through Tina." He means Ms. Needle. "She tells me that the other kids have been giving you a hard time. And I'm sorry for that too. And your mother." His shoulders slump. "Worst year ever, huh, buddy?"

Massive understatement.

"I don't want to take the risk of revealing what I've built until you're off the ship. And that day's coming soon. Today—the day I'm recording this message—is June 1st. The last day of school is in just over two weeks. My plan now is to wait it out. You'll be home in no time and then I'll feel much more comfortable telling my story to whoever wants to listen. Maybe I'll even make a buck or two."

He winks at me.

"What'ya say? Hawaii? Something more exotic? Fiji, maybe? Tahiti?"

I feel my cheeks getting hot. My dad knows me way too well.

"But like I said, if you're watching this, something's gone wrong. Maybe I've been thrown in jail or worse.

Maybe something's come after us. I don't know. But if we've been separated, I need you to hear this. To try to understand." He pauses and stares into the screen. He wants me to know that he means what he's saying. "I did this for *you*. I got the chance to give you a bigger, hopefully better world than the one I was given. So I had to take it."

My eyes are glassing over, but I don't care. Ari and Becka seeing me cry seems so tiny compared to what I'm watching.

"And in case someone bad *does* come after the 118 while you're still onboard—well—the engine I built should work just fine. In theory. I want us to make the maiden voyage together. But if I can't be there, you finish the job for me, okay?"

He holds up a hand to wave goodbye. It's an awkward gesture and I think he knows it.

"Love you, son."

The screen flickers and goes back to being a window, leaving the stars to twinkle as we drift in orbit around Elvid IV. I don't know what to say. I don't think there's anything *to* say. After hearing this recording, I have even more questions than I had before. But at the moment, the only question that matters is the one Becka asked after we ran out of gas: what now?

We're still stuck out here, and it's still mainly my fault. But I might be able to fix it.

"Becka?" I ask, wiping my eyes with my sleeve.

"Yeah?"

She uses the same I-feel-so-bad-for-you voice that the teachers have used a lot lately. But coming from her, it feels different. Becka rarely cuts anyone slack. She's letting me know she's with me. And I appreciate it.

"You're on comms and the scanner, right?"

She nods.

We can't give up. We've made it this far. And I'm the captain, I remind myself. I'm the captain.

I take a deep breath. "We're free. Out of fuel for my dad's engine. But *free*."

"I guess," Becka says. "Can't go far, though."

"But there has to be more in this solar system than whatever's on Elvid IV, right? If we can find it, maybe we can find a way to replenish the fuel supplies. Traveling faster than the speed of light may be new for *us*—"

"But *they* probably do it all the time," Ari finishes.

"Exactly," I say. "Like, maybe you can just buy quantum hexachloride at a gas station or something. Enough to make it to Ganymede and bring back help for everyone else."

"But we don't have any Elvidian money," Becka points out.

"So what?" I say. "We figured out how to get out of that jail—we'll figure out the next part too. Right now, all we need is a place to go."

Becka nods and touches her screen, swiping this way and that.

"Well, Captain," she says after a minute, totally unsarcastically, "according to my readings, the most populated planet in the solar system with—whoa—57 *billion* sentient life signs is . . . the ninth planet down from the suns." She looks up, smiling. "And it's not that far away."

I nod. That's a lot of life signs. More aliens on that one planet than there are humans in our entire solar system. I can't tell whether that means finding light speed fuel will be really easy or really hard.

"How long will it take us to get there?"

"Sending you coordinates now, Ari," Becka says.

"At top speed?" Ari answers, looking at his screen. "It won't take long. Four or five hours, maybe."

I wind through some displays on my chair's computer console, bringing up the ship's supplies. At least we have plenty of *regular* fuel. We can wander around this system for months, no problem, although I really hope it doesn't come to that.

"Good," I say. "Set a course."

16

The ship assures us that its autopilot setting can handle this linear orbit-to-orbit travel on its own—but we don't 100% trust it to stay on course without a little supervision. So we keep someone on the bridge at all times. One by one we take turns changing our clothes, showering, napping for a bit, and grabbing something to eat that isn't another bowl of Garlic O's.

We've been wearing our school uniforms for three days, ever since the end-of-the-year assembly. We don't stink or anything—our clothes are actually *cleaner* than when we were captured (which Ari thinks has something to do with the Elvidians' advanced technology). But just because my uniform is clean doesn't mean I'm not super sick of wearing it. When it's my turn to freshen up, I dig into my suitcase—which I packed the night before our last day of school—and change into a pair of jeans and a T-shirt. If I have to go on a desperate and dangerous treasure hunt to an overpopulated alien planet, I may as well be comfy. I even consider changing out of my old black sneakers and into a pair of flip-flops. But I'm too worried that I might have to run away from something or someone in the near future. Flip-flops don't feel like the right footwear for a galactic fugitive.

After I pass out for a few hours, I head over to the kitchen next to the cafeteria. Thankfully, the lunch robots are still offline. They would not appreciate us raiding what's left of their supplies. The fridges are almost empty, like they usually are at the end of the school year. (And I can't even remember the last time we got a fresh produce delivery. May? *April?*) But the pantry is still well stocked, so I make myself literally the greatest peanut butter and jelly sandwich on this side of the galaxy, topped off with all the chocolate chip cookies I can eat. Fun fact: the number of chocolate chip cookies I *can* eat is a lot more than the number of chocolate chip cookies I *should* eat. So by the time I rejoin Ari and Becka on the bridge, I'm a little nauseous.

Totally worth it.

Sitting back down in the captain's chair, I notice that Becka and Ari also changed into jeans and T-shirts. Maybe when this is all over, we can talk to Principal Lochner about easing up on the dress code. If we survive red-eyed aliens from another part of the galaxy, then we can probably handle shorts in math class. At least casual Fridays or something.

"Are we there yet?" I ask, amazed at how much

better I feel now that I've showered, slept, and eaten some real food.

"Almost," Ari answers, his fingers tapping nervously on his screen. "But—"

I spin around, my mind only half-focused on this conversation.

"Good, good. Anyone following us?"

I wonder if maybe we should bring a crate of cookies up to the bridge to have on hand when we get hungry. That would definitely be a good captainy decision.

"No, I don't think so," Ari answers. "But—"

"Great. Do we have any more information on the planet we're heading toward?"

Maybe we could wheel a whole fridge up here. Or a freezer packed with ice cream. If I ever run my own spaceship when I'm an adult, I'm going to have ice cream on the bridge all the time. Why isn't that already a thing?

"Yes. Becka's learned some things . . ."

"Awesome! What do you—"

"Jack!" Ari yells, rudely interrupting me after I've interrupted him a bunch of times. "Listen!"

"Sheesh," I say. "What is it?"

I know that things can't be classified as "great" at the moment. But we deserve a few minutes of peace before the next crisis, right?

"Becka's been scanning our surroundings," Ari explains. "And when we looked at the readings, we noticed something."

"Noticed what?" I ask.

"That's just it," Ari says, "I don't know. It's not a ship. It's not a planet. It's not anything that I recognize. It's just this . . . bubble. And it's coming up *fast*."

"A bubble," I echo.

"It completely surrounds the ninth planet."

"Like more light speed jamming?"

"No, this is something else."

"Do you think we should stop?"

"Nah," says Becka, who's casually wringing out her wet hair onto the carpet. "There are lots of ships out here now, coming and going from the planet, in and out of the bubble. And they all seem fine."

She gestures at the window, and I realize there are loads of weird-looking ships all around us. Traffic. Fifty-something billion aliens all in one place will do that, I guess. "Okay," I say. "How much longer until we get to the planet?"

"Eh, not long, I don't think," Ari answers. "At this speed, we should be there in—"

"**CHECKPOINT.**"

Ari falls silent. Becka and I freeze.

Something is out there.

"**NON-INDIGENOUS LIFE-FORMS DE-TECTED ABOARD.**"

"Do you see anything else on the scanners?" I ask Becka. "Are we under attack?"

She shrugs. "I don't think so. I mean, none of these

other ships are acting like anything's wrong."

"Did that voice come from one of the other ships?"

Becka runs a scan. "I . . . I can't tell."

"What should we do?" Ari asks. "Turn back?"

Before I can answer, a blue wall of light materializes directly in front of us, in space, and begins to move
quickly toward the ship. Toward all of the ships. I don't
know what it is. And I don't want to find out. I want
to yell to Ari—tell him throw the engines into reverse.
But there isn't time. Between our speed and the speed of
the moving light, we hit it in less than a second. I grab
the sides of the captain's chair and flinch, bracing for an
impact—

—that doesn't happen.

Instead, we just pass directly through the light. It
ripples as it moves around us and through us. It's some
kind of scan, I guess. The light touches my skin, which
tingles like a cold breeze just blew through the bridge.

It moves over Ari and Becka half a second after it
moves over me.

"**ASSESSMENT COMPLETE,**" the creepy mind-
voice booms. "**COMMENCING ORIENTATION.**"

We look at each other.

"What's—"

Pop.

* * *

"—orientation?"

A burst of blinding white light fades as quickly as it came, leaving a few lingering purple spots floating in front of me, playing tricks on my eyes. But they also vanish almost instantly and my vision adjusts . . . to my new surroundings.

We've moved.

Instead of *sitting* on the bridge of the 118, we're *standing* in a giant, single-file line that stretches out endlessly in front of us. Becka and Ari are in front of me, unharmed. I glance behind me: with each passing second, the line gets longer and longer as more aliens appear out of nowhere in the back of the line. *Pop*—another alien. *Pop*—another alien. *Pop*—another alien.

"Um, did we just teleport?" Becka asks.

"Maybe?" Ari says, halfway between a grimace and a smile. He can't help getting excited about each new discovery, no matter how terrifying.

This room is big. I think. But it isn't easy to tell *how* big. It's barely a "room" at all. There aren't any walls. There's no ceiling. And if I wasn't standing on solid ground, I'd say that there was no floor either. Everything is just . . . white. But not like the cafeteria on our ship, which has all solid white walls because of the digital paper. This feels different. Misty. Like we're in a cloud, or a dream.

I give myself the pinch test. It hurts, which seems like a good sign, but doesn't feel like enough evidence.

So I kick Becka lightly in the back of one of her legs.

"Hey!"

"Sorry," I say. "Just checking that this is real."

She kicks me back, *not* lightly.

"Ow!"

"Real enough for you?" she grunts.

So we're not in a dream. Probably. "Then where *are* we?" I ask.

Ari shrugs, and Becka says, "Your guess is as good as mine."

The line moves up a few inches, and we shimmy forward with the aliens in front of us and behind us. I look to either side. Ours isn't the only line. There must be at least a hundred others to our left and another hundred to our right—and *no one* is Elvidian: Two-legged, eight-handed, purple giraffes, with necks tied in knots? Check. Lizards with strings of light bulbs for tails? Check. Aliens that look *almost* human, except for the extra ear sticking out the tops of their heads? Check.

Creatures of all shapes and sizes, and even some *without* shapes and sizes. Blobs of light. I kid you not: tubes of dust with googly eyes.

This is one strange galaxy.

Some of the aliens around us are chatting calmly. Some are standing around silently. But—even though I assume they were also plucked from their ships with no explanation—nobody seems alarmed.

Well, almost nobody.

A booming scream fills the room and an alien shrieks—"You can't do this!"—from a few lines over.

The crowd is thick, and it's not easy to see who's shouting. But when we step forward again, I get a glimpse of her through a break in one of the lines. She's got light green skin and is wearing a dark green toga draped over one of her shoulders. She has long, sharp spikes growing out of her head, sticking out from under her green hair—which makes her look kind of like the Statue of Liberty. I glance around. She isn't the only green lady in here, but the others are all trying to ignore their distressed friend.

"No!" she screams to no one in particular, like she's talking to some invisible person in the sky. "Please! I forgot about Orientation! I can't go through it again!"

She's huffing and puffing and spinning around in place, shouting at the non-existent roof. Most of the other aliens in line are pretending she isn't here. She's the only one freaking out.

"I don't want to go! I'm just here to get some supplies for my family! Please! And I love the Minister already. I won't say anything bad about her while I'm planetside. I promise! I won't even *think* anything bad about her!"

Even though she's the only one who seems bothered by this place, she doesn't sound like she's gone off the deep end. She just sounds . . . *scared*.

"Just send me back!" she begs. "I don't want to go to the planet anymore! I don't need the supplies that badly.

I've changed my mind! So just send me back! Do you hear me! *Send me back!*"

Standing up on my tiptoes, I can finally see what's at the end of each line: small, square, glass booths. They're staffed by Elvidians wearing plain black uniforms who stare at aliens passing in front of the booths one by one. This place reminds me of the trip I took with my parents to the European Zone on Mars. It was a few years ago, before they got divorced, and my mom had a doctor convention there. When we walked from the American side to the Eurozone, we had to go through something similar.

"I think this is, like, passport control," I whisper to Ari and Becka.

I start to sweat. We don't have any IDs on us. And if the Elvidians at the front figure out who we are, we'll be dragged back to Elvid IV, or worse.

We're close to the front of our line now. I watch as aliens approach the glass booth one at a time. A bluish light (the same shade as the one that scanned the ship) shines down for a few seconds. The Elvidian in the booth says something. The aliens step forward—and disappear into the white, misty walls that surround us.

"No!" the woman from the other line shrieks again. She's reached the front. "I can't! I won't!"

But she doesn't have much choice. Two armored Elvidian guards approach and drag her toward the booth, holding each of her arms. As the blue light passes over her, the guards swing her backward and toss her into the white mist, mid-scream.

"Next!" the Elvidian at the end of our line shouts. Add that to the growing list of things Elvidians are obsessed with: sitting behind desks while shouting "Next!" to frightened people.

Now it's Ari's turn. He glances around, and I know what he's searching for: a way out. But there isn't any. So, trembling, Ari walks up to the glass booth as the room scans him.

"Don't turn around," says a voice in my ear. The alien behind me is whispering to me. And I know: when an alien whispers "don't turn around," you don't turn around. But I can't help it. My heads whips to the side to see . . . no one. Or no one standing immediately behind me, anyway. There's a line of aliens back there, of course. But the closest one—a little Statue of Liberty—is chatting with another alien, using a voice that sounds nothing like the one I just heard.

"I said not to turn around," the voice rumbles. "You will arouse suspicion."

I face front.

The guard says a few words to Ari, who throws a worried look back at us before stepping forward into the wall and disappearing.

"I can speak directly to you—into your mind—but only in this waystation," the voice in my ear contin- ues. "You should not have come here. But now that you have, I will do the only thing I can for you and tell you this: It isn't real. It's terrifying. And different for everyone. But it isn't real."

"Next!"

Becka's turn. She walks up to the booth . . .

"And it will get to you eventually if you keep returning here, which I strongly advise against."

The Elvidian guard speaks again, and Becka takes one fearless stride into the mist.

"They'll try to make you love the Minister," the mind voice tells me. "But it isn't real. You can't be brainwashed if you remember that. It isn't real."

"Next!"

I hesitate, wanting to question whoever is speaking to me. But there isn't time. So I whisper, "Okay," and walk forward.

The blue light shines on me.

"Distrusting, level five," the Elvidian guard says in a monotone. He blows a bubble with the gum he's chewing. "Approval-seeking, level three. Abandonment-fearing, level seven. Long live the Minister. Welcome to Elvid IX. Enjoy your visit."

"Thanks?" I say, confused and scared.

"Proceed," the Elvidian orders.

I look ahead of me, seeing nothing but a swirling cloud of white, and step into the mist.

17

"Jack," Ari says. "Will you pass me that Pencil over there?"

"Ari? What—what happened? How did we get back here?"

We're on the PSS 118, sitting in our regular seats in history class. The lights are dimmer than usual and the only desks in the room are mine and Ari's. But everything else seems totally normal.

"Back here?" Ari asks. "What do you mean? And will you *please* pass me that Pencil over there?"

He gestures toward a shelf behind me, where a Pencil leans against a few textbooks.

"Sure," I say, handing him the nanoprinter and looking around. "Where's Becka?"

He smiles and sighs. "She is just *perfect*."

"Right. Not my question."

"But she is," he insists, fiddling with the Pencil, clicking and writing in the air. "Absolutely, perfectly, perfect. Can you even believe how incredible she is?"

"I know, I know. She's great."

Typical.

He grins as he continues coding. "I'm going to make a picture of her!"

"Aha." On second thought, maybe Ari *is* acting a little weirder than usual.

"It won't do her justice," he goes on. "She's so beautiful. Her eyes. Her face. And that voice! Have you ever heard anything so angelic?"

"Angelic?"

The man has *lost* it.

That's when the door to the classroom swings wide open and Becka charges into the room.

"Isn't she perfect?" Ari asks, smiling up at Becka.

Oh man. I want to look away. It's like watching a space wreck happen in slow motion.

"Perfect," Becka agrees. "She is just *perfect*."

Wait, who are they talking about?

"Guys," I say. "What's going on?"

"She's perfect," Becka and Ari creepily say at the exact same time, like possessed twins in a horror movie. "An angel."

"*Who?*" I shout—but before the question leaves my lips, I realize that I already know the answer. I don't remember what happened during Orientation. One second, I was walking into the mist, and the next, I'm back here. But Becka and Ari must have been brainwashed.

"The Minister," they answer dreamily, their voices in total sync.

"You're not thinking straight," I say, hoping that I can break whatever spell they're under. "The Elvidians did something to you. You don't really think that the Minister is perfect. We've never even *met* the Minister."

Ari gasps and Becka starts cracking her knuckles.

"Not . . . perfect . . . ?" Becka asks, grinding her teeth. "Take it back!"

As she marches toward me, I jump up from my chair and back away. She pauses under a bright light that casts a long shadow over the classroom.

"Hold on, Becka. Relax. This isn't you." I look at her red face and tightly closed fists. "Well, okay, this is kind of you. But not really."

"How dare you insult the Minister!" She raises a fist and moves to punch me into the face.

"Whoa!" I shout, ducking just in time.

Her fist connects with the wall behind me, *making a hand-shaped dent in the plaster.* She spins around to face me, her eyes wild with hate. That alien mysterious voice wasn't kidding. Orientation really does a number on you. But how did they get affected so badly while I got out okay?

"No!" Ari shouts to Becka, squeezing between her and me. I'm glad that he's coming to his senses—until I watch him clench *his* fists with the same rage. "Let me."

What?

"Take it back," he commands. "Tells us that you love her."

"What? No! Listen, they *did* something to you. You've got to snap out of it. We've got to refuel that engine. The Minister—"

"The Minister!" Becka interrupts.

"The Minister!" Ari repeats. "Long live the Minister! Long live the Minister!"

He clicks the Pencil, still in his hand, and out pops a large picture in a fancy frame, with brush strokes like a museum oil painting. The picture is of an Elvidian woman—red eyes, white hair, sharp nails—holding a scepter made of lasers and sitting on a shimmering black throne. Now *that's* an alien queen. It's like she knows that Elvidians already kind of look like fairy tale monsters and has decided to embrace it. As soon as the image appears, Ari and Becka bow down to the floor.

"Long live the Minister," they say over and over. "Long live the Minister."

"Stop it!" I shout, staring down at Ari. "Please. I'm your friend, remember? Your *best* friend. You have to listen to me. We—we need to do something."

He slowly rises up, squinting at me with flared nostrils.

"You're right," he says.

But the way he says it . . . it's all wrong.

Becka gets up and stands next to him, the floating picture of the Minister hovering between their shoulders.

"Yes," she says. "We need to do *something*."

The two of them step closer to me.

"Something needs to change," Ari says. "If you don't love her—if you don't *believe* in her—we can't be friends anymore." He says it as if this is the most obvious thing in the world. "In fact, we've never really been friends."

"What? You can't think that's true."

"I think all sorts of things now," he says. "Like how you've always made fun of me for liking Becka." I look over at her, waiting for *some* reaction. But nothing. Not even a blink. They're both total zombies. "For thinking that I'm not good enough for her."

"That's not—"

"No!" he barks.

Becka sidesteps over to him and grabs his hand. They interlock their fingers.

"No," he says again. "You don't believe in me. You think I'm a joke. But I'm not listening to you anymore. You're not smarter than me. Not more important than me. *No one* likes you."

"Not me," Becka volunteers.

"And not me," Ari says. "I've felt bad for you. Because your mom left and your dad went nuts being around you. But just because you're a loser doesn't mean we have to be friends. I deserve better. Better than you."

"Ari," I choke. "Think about what you're saying. Please."

He laughs and it gives me goosebumps. How am I

going to fix this? I know he doesn't mean it. But still . . . maybe he's not totally off base. I've always made fun of him for his crush on Becka (which *is* ridiculous, isn't it?). I've barely paid attention to him lately (but I had an excuse, didn't I?). And Doctor Shrew . . . I mean . . . I was under a lot of stress and . . .

No. That was unforgiveable.

And maybe everything else was too.

"Good-bye," Ari says, wrapping his arm around Becka. "See ya never."

They leave the room and I'm left by myself, clueless and terrified and sad. I don't even call out after them. I just stand there, staring into the red-eyed face of the Minister in the floating picture in front of me.

What do I do?

I close my eyes and reopen them a second later.

* * *

"Jack," Ari says. "Will you pass me that Pencil over there?"

Wait. What?

We're back in the history room. The books are stacked neatly on the shelf, Becka is nowhere in sight, and the floating image of the Minister is gone.

"Ari?" I ask.

"That's me," he says. "Now will you *please* pass me that Pencil over there?"

I look behind me and, sure enough, the Pencil is exactly where it was a few minutes ago. My mind is racing. What's happening? Where did Becka go? Why are we here again? It's like life just rewound itself.

And it hits me.

I thought that the brainwashing hadn't worked on me. That I had come out of Orientation fine and that Ari and Becka had been reprogrammed. But I was wrong. I haven't come out of Orientation at all.

This *is* Orientation.

It must be some sort of . . . simulation. Not real, just like the voice said. I'm a little relieved, and a little afraid, and really don't want to experience all that again. But I don't have a choice. And it goes almost as it did before, except this time, it ends with me on the floor, having been tripped by Orientation Becka, while Orientation Ari does a clumsy slow dance with the painting of the Minister. Becka's cackling like a madwoman, Ari looks like he's about to plant one on the canvas Minister, and I squeeze my eyes shut again. And again. And again.

* * *

Sometimes it ends with me getting made fun of. Once or twice, they beat me up. There's this one version where I poke a hole in the painting, which makes them both cry. And sometimes, when I'm too mentally exhausted to resist, I pretend to agree. Tell them what they want to hear. That the Minister is perfect. That I love her and believe in her. By the twentieth or thirtieth or fortieth time, I forget—for a few seconds—that this is a simulation and that I'm not talking to the real Ari and Becka. Maybe I should consider trusting and loving the Minister. If they like her so much, she can't be all that bad, right?

I blink.

* * *

"Jack? Jack!"

It's Ari's voice.

"Come on, Jack, wake up."

That's Becka.

"You don't want me to pour water on you again, do you?"

My mind clears and I force my eyes open. We're back on the bridge of the ship and I'm sitting in the captain's chair, just as I was before Orientation. But are we really back? How do I know this isn't just another trick?

I look over at Ari, who seems absolutely exhausted. I can see it in his eyes.

"You okay?" I ask him.

He squints in my direction and bites the inside of his cheek.

"Yeah," he says, like he's scared of me. I wonder what Orientation Jack was like. Not great, I assume. "You?"

"Yeah, fine. What about you, Becka? You all right?"

It's weird. Toward the end, I could feel myself giving in. Getting lost. But now . . . now, it's different. It's like remembering a movie you saw a long time ago. A terrible movie. But a movie, not a memory.

Becka stares at me without blinking—and tilts her head weirdly, straining her neck as far as it'll bend.

"Long live the Minister," she says robotically. "Long live the Minister."

"No," Ari whispers.

She looks at him and smiles coldly.

"I don't understand," Ari says, turning to me in a panic. "Why is she still like this? Are we . . . am I . . . still inside?"

Oh no. If the brainwashing worked on her—if Becka still believes all the things it made her believe—I don't know how we'll ever win her back. And if we're still inside Orientation . . . I'm not sure how much more I can take.

"Long live the . . . gotcha!"

Ari and I look at each other. "What?" I yell.

Becka lets out a snort of laughter. "You should've seen your faces."

Ari's hyperventilating. He slumps down into his chair.

"That *wasn't* funny," I tell her. "How could you . . ."

And that's when I look at her. Really look. She's smiling and her hands are resting confidently on her waist. But in and around her eyes, that telltale Becka strength is sapped. She's as shaken as Ari and I. Maybe more. She isn't messing with us for fun. She's coping.

"Let's just focus," I say. Yelling more at Becka doesn't seem right. We need to put this behind us. It's over. "What time is it?"

I look at my reflection in the glass of the window in front of me and then back at Ari and Becka. I don't look any different. Neither do they. We aren't *older*. At least, I don't think we are. But my Orientation lasted a long time. And I have a feeling that theirs did too.

"How much time passed while we were in there?" I ask Ari.

Ari looks down at his screen. "Four," he mumbles.

"Four what?" I ask. "Days?"

He doesn't answer.

"*Weeks?*"

Did it all happen in real time?

He looks up at me, all the color gone from his face.

"Four seconds," he answers. "Just four seconds."

18

Now that we're through the Orientation bubble, it doesn't take long to reach our destination: Elvid IX. (We humans may not be the most advanced species in the galaxy, but at least we give our planets decent names. "Earth," "Mars," and "Jupiter" have a lot more pizzazz than "Human Planet 3," "Human Planet 4," and "Human Planet 5," right?)

Ari brings us in close to the giant ringed planet. He's not a half-bad pilot—but he's not a full-good pilot either. That's understandable, I guess, seeing as he's thirteen and doesn't really know how to fly a ship. We only do two unintentional barrel rolls as we head into orbit.

"Meant to do that," Ari lies both times, clenching his teeth.

It's a rule: Everything looks epic from space. But up close, Elvid IX is an eyesore. It's one endless city from pole to pole, packed with sky-high, rounded smokestacks that spew pillars of soot into the air. And it's overcrowded with swarms of ships doing the same thing from their exhaust lines. Pro tip: Don't take any deep breaths on Elvid IX. No shallow breaths either. Don't even hiccup.

Becka's scans tell her that the hazy atmosphere is toxic from all the pollution. And even though it's daytime on this side of the planet, it's dark as night down here. The air is so thick and dirty that it literally blots out the suns.

"Welcome to Nine," the Minister tells us. "Pride of the galaxy."

I yelp, Ari falls off his chair, and Becka snorts like a bull about to charge—until she looks down at her display.

"Just a recording," she explains. "It started downloading when we entered the atmosphere."

Just like in the floating picture from my Orientation, the Minister is holding her laser stick and sitting on her throne. She's wearing a shiny black robe that looks cut from whatever the buildings are made out of on Elvid IV. And she does not look friendly.

"Can you turn it off?" I ask.

"Nope," Becka answers. "It's playing by itself."

"Whether you are visiting for business or leisure," the Minister continues, "you have made the right choice. If Nine doesn't have it, it doesn't exist. Your ship's data bank should now have access to a free public map— including of our planet and many of its most prominent landmarks—along with an Elvidian dictionary that should be fully compatible with all internal reading systems. While here, you absolutely must see the sights: the tallest statue in the galaxy—"

"A thousand bucks says the statue's of her," Becka mutters.

"—the largest shopping mall in existence, the Great Nine Zoo, and, of course, the First Elvidian Mines. And that's just the beginning. But remember," the Minister adds, leaning forward on her throne, "always be on the lookout for miscreants and disruptors. Not everyone in the galaxy is as *civilized* as the Elvidian people and those we dutifully serve. We need *you* to keep us safe and secure."

"Welcome to Nine," she says again. "Long live the Minister."

The recording cuts off as we dip below the clouds.

"Did she just 'long live' *herself*?" Becka says.

I chuckle, mostly out of relief that the recording is over. I don't think I'll ever be able to hear "Long live the Minister" again without reliving the memory of Orientation Ari and Orientation Becka. It's not pleasant.

"What now?" Ari asks as we fly around one rising column of smoke after another.

I still don't love the Minister. But she makes a good point.

"You heard her. We absolutely must see the sights."

***

"I thought we were going to the zoo," Ari grumbles.

"I doubt there's fuel at the zoo," I point out. He touches us down inside the mall's parking lot and finds an open space between a purple egg rocket and a ship that looks like a mechanical butterfly.

The mall is shaped like a pyramid with a smokestack at the top. A smooth volcano, I guess, with flat sides and sharp edges. The pyramid's surface is a giant billboard: every inch of it is covered with flashy advertisements, bright enough that you can see them through the smog from pretty far out. My digital contacts are doing a decent job translating the Elvidian words—at least for basic stuff like tables and jetpacks and ships.

But eighty percent of the ads still make no sense to me. What's "THERMOWAVE EXOLINING"? And why would anybody need "SEVEN FLOORS OF SHREDDED HAND TOWELS"? That last one's got to be a mistranslation. Then again, maybe not. According to the map that auto-downloaded into the 118's data bank, the mall is over seven hundred stories tall. So it might literally sell *everything*.

"Where's the fuel?" Ari asks.

Becka forwarded a copy of the map to her ring and is now staring at a miniature rotating hologram of the mall in her palm.

"Gimme a second," she answers, turning the map halfway around and zooming in.

Ari powers down the engines and a tunnel

automatically extends from the walls of the parking garage. It moves toward one of the ship's main entrances and seals itself against the door like a jetway attaching to a commercial spaceliner.

"Got it," Becka says a second later, holding out her hand. A small green blip is flashing toward the top of the pyramid. "There are two stores up on one of the high floors that both sell fuel for light speed engines." She looks back down at her hand and swipes some more. "But forget that for a sec. There's a lot of cool stuff in here."

"Like what?" Ari asks.

"Later," I interrupt, shaking my head. "First we get fuel. Then *maybe* we can explore."

"Don't be boring," Becka tells me, swiping from one level of the mall to another. "There's a zero-g restaurant, a cloning store, an arcade—"

"With alien video games?" Ari spurts out. "Like what?"

Becka accesses the listing and scrolls through. "Um, a lot of flight simulators. Some sports stuff. Skee-ball, maybe? And there's a time machine, I think."

"A *what?!*"

She reads more. "A time machine. Can take you back up to a couple days. Looks like there are a lot of rules, though."

Ari turns to me. "We *have* to go."

"We *have* to do what we came here to do," I tell him.

I'm not being boring, right? I mean, we're here for a reason. We can't afford to be irresponsible.

"Maybe we can go later," I say.

"It's a *time machine*," Ari explains, shaking with excitement. He grabs me by the collar of my T-shirt. "We can go *earlier*."

I don't even know what that means. "We'll go, okay? I promise. But first let's find the fuel. Please. I need to know we can get home."

Ari sighs and lets go of me. "Fine. As long as you promise."

"I promise. And in the meantime, any ideas on how we can buy fuel without any money?"

"We could ask nicely," Ari says sincerely, as the three of us leave the bridge and head toward the exit hatch. "Explain that we need it to get home."

"We could steal it," Becka suggests, ignoring Ari's suggestion.

I roll my eyes at her.

"What?" she asks, shrugging. We step through the tunnel and into the mall. "We're criminals, aren't we? And like you said, we've done well so far."

"We've been lucky," I say. And luck runs out eventually.

19

Money's always been tight in the Graham house: Everything I'm wearing is a hand-me-down. My parents only ever give me Christmas/birthday combo presents (even though my birthday's in June). And I've never even been to a real mall. Shopping's not really our thing.

But even if I had visited one of the malls on Ganymede, nothing could have prepared me for *this*.

"Is that a dragon?" Ari asks.

We've entered the mall through a tunnel from the parking garage and are now standing outside the weirdest pet shop ever. Becka has been studying the map to get our bearings, but Ari's question sidetracks her. He's staring up at a massive aquarium in the front window.

"Technically"—Becka snickers, checking the map "I'm not making this up, I swear. According to the translation, they're giant sea monsters.'"

I glance at the aquarium, which is bigger than my dorm room on the 118. At first, it looks empty, except for some pebbles and fake plants, as if it's galaxy's biggest goldfish bowl. But as I squint to see through the murky water at the back of the tank . . . *BAM!* A truck-sized sea dragon—with sharp teeth, silvery scales, and pointy claws—rams its slimy face against the glass. It does it again, staring out at us like it could use a snack.

I jump back. "Okay, guys, no more distractions. Let's go find that fuel."

But Ari and Becka are already heading into the store.

"Hey!" I call out, trailing after them. "Wait up! And—"

My ring chimes with a text. Another hidden message from my dad? I open my palm and flip my hand: No name. No time stamp. No location. Just three words: "You must leave."

So not my dad this time. But every bit as urgent and mysterious. I think about the voice I heard before Orientation—wondering if this is the same person—and type back: "Who are you?" But the ring just tells me that THIS MESSAGE CANNOT BE DELIVERED.

Distracted, I walk straight into Ari.

"Huh?" he turns around. "What is it? What's wrong?"

I make a split-second decision and close my hand. "Nothing," I answer. "Sorry. Nothing."

"Excellent choice," a nearby Elvidian says, talking to some other customers in the store. He's crouching down on a small hovering platform, fishing something out from the top of another aquarium. He's wearing goggles, thick gloves, and a white smock with the word "Wrangler" printed on the front. His long fingers are wrapped tight around a pole with a mechanical claw at the end, which he's swirling around inside the tank.

Becka and Ari watch him in fascination, but I'm lost in my thoughts about the text. About who could've sent it and what it might mean. Someone wants us to leave. Leave the mall? Leave Elvid IX? Leave this solar system? I mean, we *will* leave as soon as we get the fuel for our light speed engine. But unless the messenger wants to lend us some Elvidian credits to buy quantum hexachloride, they're not being very helpful.

The hovering wrangler is still talking to two other Elvidians on the ground—one tall, the other short. Maybe a dad and a kid? "These are substantially more docile than the Tacanite breed, although they are some of the fastest-growing creatures we stock."

"You sure this is the one you want, honey?" asks the taller Elvidian shopper.

"Yes! Yes!" snaps his kid.

"The Tacanites look more powerful, though," the dad says, gesturing toward the scarier silvery monster across the aisle. He knocks on the glass to get the angry one's attention. "Look at those teeth."

"I want *this* one!" the kid whines, jumping up and down. "*This* one!"

The dad slumps over, disappointed. "Fine. But it's

your responsibility. I don't want to have to come back here tomorrow because you forgot to feed it."

Should I tell the others about the message? *I'd* want to know if *they'd* gotten a mysterious text. On the other hand, what good would it do?

The wrangler sways back and forth on his platform and clumsily plucks a small dragon out of the tank. It looks pretty friendly. It has colorful scales and short arms that end in smooth dolphin flippers, instead of sharp claws. And as the sea monster is lifted out of the tank, it leaves behind a swirling trail of purple and blue, like it's shedding skin made out of glitter.

"We have a six-cycle warranty with a full, money-back guarantee," the wrangler explains. "You'd have to pass a basic lie detection examination, of course. To make sure your loss was not purposeful. Dragon fraud is a serious problem."

He pulls the creature out of the water and lowers himself to the ground. As he descends, we get a good look at the full-grown versions of the baby he's holding in the claw. They're as giant as the mean one behind us, but they're doing happy cartwheels underwater instead of giving us the hungry-eye.

No. I'm not going to tell them. It won't change anything—it'll only worry and confuse them. More than we're all already worried and confused.

Besides, I'm the captain. It's my call.

"A few more things you may already know," the

wrangler continues, plopping the baby sea monster down into a bowl on the floor. "This little Strykor will be fully matured in a few hours—"

"*Hours?*" Ari whispers to himself.

"—so transfer it to much, much larger accommodations as soon as possible. Growth spurts can be sudden and substantial, especially after a feeding. He's a vegetarian, more or less. But Strykors can get aggressive if they're not fed often. And they can survive for at least fifteen minutes outside the water. So it's recommended that you keep him in a well-sealed tank for containment purposes."

Both the kid and the dad are nodding like this is all perfectly normal information, as if they're well prepared to house and feed a soon-to-be-giant sea monster that can get "aggressive" and is only "more or less" a vegetarian. They finish their purchase: the worker cuts off a yellow band tied around the monster's fin ("For security.") and hands over the dragon bowl and a triangle piece of plastic ("Your receipt.").

"We should go," I tell Ari and Becka. "Please? Becka, you've figured out where we are by now, right?"

"Level 650," she replies. "The fuel stores are on level 341."

"All right, let's get moving." We start to follow the dad and his kid toward the exit, where the store opens up to the main atrium of the mall—but the wrangler gets in our way.

"And what about you?" he asks, adjusting his goggles.

"Just browsing? Or can I interest you in a Pomona? Maybe a hybrid Skir?"

"No thanks," I answer, at the exact same time Ari says, "Sure!"

"No thanks," Becka agrees, pulling Ari along by his shirt.

"Well, do come again," the Elvidian calls after us.

Suddenly, from somewhere outside the store, we hear a crash—like glass shattering—and shouting that we can't make out. A second later, the dad and kid come walking back in. The kid is sopping-wet and empty-handed. No baby dragon in sight.

"Excuse me," the dad says, handing back the plastic triangle. "About that warranty?"

The wrangler scowls, leading them toward the back of the store, while we finally make our exit.

* * *

The mall is packed. It's mostly Elvidian shoppers—maybe nineteen out of every twenty—but there are other aliens too: some Statues of Liberty, some velociraptors in tuxedos. And there are long lines everywhere, crisscrossing the floor and looping around a big circular fountain in the middle.

"Okay," I say. "How do we get down to level 341?"

"We could walk," Becka suggests, pointing out a spiral staircase near the fountain. "Or race!"

Becka's already bouncing up and down on her toes. She lives her whole life like someone's about to blow the whistle on the start of a marathon.

"Race down *three hundred* flights of stairs?" Ari asks.

Becka tilts her head to the side and cracks her neck. "Yep."

"No thanks," I say, spotting a quicker—but not necessarily less scary—way down: glass cylinders, scattered around the floor. They look like the tubes from Io's underground subways. Only these are different. Emptier. There are no train cars here. These are more like one-person elevators, without the elevator.

We get in line for the cylinder with the shortest wait. We're behind an Elvidian lady dressed in a purple onesie and a half-rhino/half-goat wearing a flower-patterned shirt.

The Elvidian steps inside the tube and says "Three ninety-seven," as its doors close behind her. She doesn't even flinch as the floor opens up beneath her feet and she disappears like a bowling ball falling down a garbage chute.

"I changed my mind," Ari says, gulping. "Why don't we take the stairs? Stairs are good. I love stairs. Long live the stairs." He salutes.

"I changed my mind too," Becka shoots back. "This looks *much* more fun."

The rhinogoat squeezes into the cylinder. But he's a little too big and it takes him a minute to shove his entire body inside. "Six eighty-five," he says uncomfortably.

The doors slide shut onto his back and he has to shimmy around a few times before he can totally fit. But once the doors close completely, the top of the cylinder opens above him—and he shoots up the tube like he's being sucked up by a vacuum cleaner.

Becka instantly follows the rhinogoat into the elevator. "Three forty-one!"

She wiggles her fingers to us in a silly wave and plummets down, screaming with what I hope is joy.

"It'll be fine," I tell Ari. He's frozen solid and I need to physically push him inside the tube. "It'll be fine."

"Hurry up," another rhinogoat groans from behind me.

"We're going, we're going," I tell him.

Ari gulps—"Three forty-one"—and down he goes.

My turn. "Three forty-one, please."

Ever watch a cartoon set in a world where gravity only kind of applies? Where a character is walking along when, all of a sudden, the floor disappears and—because it takes him a second to realize the floor is gone and because he's a cartoon—it *also* takes him a second to actually fall? That's sort of what this feels like.

The landing's soft, at least, and the doors open back up to—

"Step right up! Try your hand at what has been confirmed to be the hardest game in the galaxy! Two hundred years old and never beaten!"

"Two-for-one Kerulian Combat! Free limb replacement with every dismemberment!"

"Attention, attention: if you left a flamethrower inside the Hologram of Horrors, please contact the nearest robotic attendant. Repeat: if you left—"

I look over at Becka, who's beaming at Ari, who's beaming at, well, everything. I get in Becka's face.

"This isn't the fuel floor, is it?"

"What gave it away?" she jokes, pushing me to the side. There's a giant spinning "ARCADE" sign hovering above our heads. We're surrounded by bright lights and loud noises. A lot of laughing. Even more shrieking (the good kind *and* the bad kind).

"I want to get out of here too," Becka tells me. "Get the fuel and get everybody rescued ASAP. Diana is still stuck in that jail. But she's not going anywhere. None of the 118ers are. A few more hours isn't going to make any difference. I mean, we deserve to be kids for like five minutes, don't we? I was supposed to go to camp this year! And instead . . ."

She trails off.

Instead, she found herself halfway across the galaxy inside a nightmare dreamscape that tried to brainwash her into loving a mean-eyed alien queen. I know the feeling.

Ari grabs my arm. "Come on," he says. "Five minutes. Please? Just five minutes. *Alien videogames,*" he adds, whispering the words like they're the most precious in the universe. "We're not gonna get caught. No one knows we're here."

Except maybe someone does. But—

"Fine," I agree, gritting my teeth. Maybe they're right. And either way, I didn't make a copy of the map for myself. Only Becka can get us around. "Five minutes."

Ari nods and uses his own ring to set a timer. Like a dog let loose from his leash in the park, he bolts around the room, zigzagging from one "game" to another: "Mech Attack" (where you sit inside a robot exoskeleton and bash other robots to bits), "Mind Wars" (where you attach sensors to your forehead and control small, laser-equipped drones with your brain), "Healthy Mix-and-Match" (where you combine the DNA of weird veggies to make something even weirder—we pocket a few free samples).

I can't pretend that this place isn't awesome. But we have a mission.

"One more," he says, glancing at the timer. He's got two minutes left. "Then we can go."

Ari walks over to two Elvidians waiting in the line for Mech Attack. "Excuse me. Where's the time machine?"

They shrug and he quickly moves on.

"Sorry," he says to a Statue of Liberty, "where's the time machine?"

She says something in a language that sounds *almost* like Spanish and we realize that she isn't wearing a translation bracelet. I tap my foot impatiently. As soon as Ari's timer goes off, I'm dragging him and Becka out of here.

"Hey, do you know where the time machine is?" Ari asks another Elvidian.

"Over there," she answers, pointing straight ahead. "Next to the booth where you throw bean bags into tiny black holes."

Ari's eyes go wide as he takes off. And within seconds, we're standing at the back of a short line behind a smooth metal box, maybe ten feet tall and ten feet across. It hisses with steam as one side lifts open and a mid-sized rhinogoat unstraps himself from a chair in the center.

"When am I?" he asks the crowd, before burping. Everyone chuckles. "Just kidding."

One by one, aliens enter the box and sit down. The hatch closes, the machine hisses, the hatch opens back up—and a different alien steps out.

"Okay," Ari says, "I think I get it. You go back in time inside the machine to this exact spot—so the people going in now are popping out in the past right here. And the people popping out now stood on this line in the future."

Above the metal box is a sign with a ton of writing on it. It starts big at the top and gets smaller and smaller until I can't read it anymore. I squint to take in as much as I can:

WELCOME TO THE TIME CANNON.

Five tokens for one six-hour trip. Ten for a day. Twenty for two.

RULES: Do not ride if you are pregnant or have been pregnant within the amount of time being traveled. Do not ride if you were born within the amount of time being traveled. Repeated riding may induce nausea, extreme eye watering, and/or cracks in the space-time continuum. NO SPECULATIVE FINANCIAL TRANSACTIONS MAY BE PLACED UNTIL YOU HAVE NATURALLY RETURNED TO THE PRESENT. GAMBLING WINS—INCLUDING BUT NOT LIMITED TO LOTTERIES AND SPORTS BETS—SHALL BE NULL AND VOID.

The Time Cannon is provided "AS IS." The Elvidian Shopping Authority will not be held responsible for lost memories, uncreated personal milestones, or actions that inadvertently cause the very effect sought to be avoided. Do not exit the mall before you have naturally returned to the present. CONFRONTING YOURSELF IN AN OVERLAPPING TIME STREAM IS STRICTLY PROHIBITED. The Time Cannon is not intended for political assassinations, undoing of significant historical events, or undertaking more educational assignments/examinations than would otherwise be feasible for a single individual. By riding the Time Cannon, you agree to indemnify the Elvidian Shopping Authority from any future or past third-party claims, illogical timeline loops, and/or unforeseen butterfly effects. Some alternate universes may result.

"This looks awesome," Ari says.

"Does it?" I ask.

I re-read the sign just as Ari's ring bleeps and a tiny hologram pops up out of his hand, showing us that five minutes have passed.

"Well," I say. "It's time. Let's go."

Ari shakes his head. "We should stay!"

I open my mouth to protest, but he puts up a hand and explains.

"We could *use* this. I mean, you only wanted to spend five minutes here. What if we can spend *negative* a day here? Buy us some extra time. Start looking for fuel even before we've escaped the jail. Then we'll for sure not get caught. Because we won't have escaped yet!"

Which I only maybe half understand. But it doesn't matter. "We don't have any tokens," I remind Ari. "We don't have any anything."

He leans over the shoulder of the alien who's next in line: an Elvidian who's holding a pile of small, round coins in his hand.

Ari reaches into his pocket, pulls out a Pencil, and starts writing. It's not hard to guess what he's about to try.

"I don't know if that's a good idea," I say.

"Worth a shot!"

Becka nods at him. "I like the way you think."

This is exactly why we shouldn't have come down here. I get that he believes this could help us. But it's not worth the risk. We're going to get thrown back in jail before we've even tried to refuel the ship.

Ari clicks, and out pops a handful of counterfeit tokens, the Minister's face carved on both sides. He hands a bunch of coins to Becka and me.

"*Now* we're criminals," Becka says happily.

We reach the front of the line, a foot away from the steaming metal box.

"Tokens," says a robot squatting on the floor. It's got six legs and even more eyes. "Tokens."

"Um, here you go," Ari offers, handing over the fake coins. The robot tosses them into its mouth and starts biting down.

"Evaluating," it says, talking and chewing at the same time. "Evaluating." And finally—"*Blech.*" The robot spits out a lump of bent and slimy metal onto Ari's shoes. "Fakes. Please. You think you're the only greedy kids with a nanoprinter?" It spits again and uses one of its six claws to scrape some rust off its robot tongue. "And a cheap one too. Blech. Blech."

"Come on," Ari says. "Please let us in."

"You're lucky I'm not going to report you," the robot says. "No tokens, no Time Cannon."

"How do we get tokens?" Ari asks.

"Money," it says, like we didn't already know the answer. "Not much you can do here without money."

"But where do we *get* money?"

The robot—who had been standing on four legs

before, low to the ground—gets up onto its two back ones and starts laughing in Ari's face.

"I don't know, kid. Get a job? There are a few token-taker shifts open here in the arcade. But they pay so badly that it'd take you years to earn enough for even *one* token." Its head spins completely around. "Great, now you're holding up the line—there's a Setti waiting two days in the future whose tokens I'm going to have to refund if things don't get moving."

The robot grabs the backs of our shirts with three of its hands and yanks us to the side. At the same time, it holds out a fourth hand to take someone else's tokens. Ari looks pretty disappointed—but there's a plus; I think the arcade is finally out of his system.

I sigh. "Can we go now?"

20

In the time it takes us to head upstairs, I get two more texts to my ring: "Leave this place" and "Go, now."

"What do you want?" is all I've been able to text back without Ari and Becka noticing. And again: THIS MESSAGE CANNOT BE DELIVERED.

I put the texts out of my mind. Stay focused, Jack.

"You sure we're in the right place?" I ask Becka, worried she's led us off course *again*.

Because this level of the mall is in bad shape: Flickering lights (the spooky kind, not the arcade kind). Sparks shooting out from exposed wires in a crumbling ceiling. And water all over the floor. Like the other two levels we've visited, this one has a fountain in the center. But it's bone dry and cracked clean down the middle. The debris-filled puddles all around us are so dirty that the water looks black.

A dozen robots push mops back and forth, collecting pieces of the broken roof in a portable dumpster.

But they're barely making a dent.

"I'm sure," Becka says, triple-checking her map.

Ari points to a sign that's dangling sideways above a nearby store—*Fuel! Fuel! Fuel!*—and another sign at the opposite end of the atrium—*Fuel Emporium.* We're definitely in the right place. They've just had a rough day. Or maybe an awesome party.

"You again?" an alien shouts, staring at me from underneath the *Fuel! Fuel! Fuel!* sign. She looks almost human, except for her bright purple skin and orange hair.

I stop in my tracks and glance around. "Me?" I ask, pointing to myself.

"Yes, *you*," she points back. "What do you want?"

"Uh, fuel? For a light speed engine?"

"Oh, *now* you want fuel? You haven't ruined me enough for one day?"

She turns her head left and right, waving her arms at the few shoppers slowly trudging in and out of stores. They all look a little worse for wear.

"You scared everyone away!"

"What's she talking about?" Becka mutters.

"I don't think I am who you think I am," I tell her. "This is literally the first time I've ever been here."

She squints at me and slumps her shoulders. She's got a tag on her shirt that my digital contacts can't seem to translate. It only says: *My name is* [UNKNOWN NAME].

"Oh," says UNKNOWN NAME, rubbing her eyes, "I guess you're right. I'm a little jumpy. Those overpriced hooligans over at Fuel Emporium are messing with me again. They set this whole thing up. I'm sure of it."

"Well," I say, hoping to get the conversation back on track, "we do need some fuel."

UNKNOWN NAME clasps her hands together.

"You've come to the right place," she cheers, leading us into her store. "I'm glad you decided to avoid those *crooks*"—she says the word at the top of her lungs, like she wants everyone on the floor to hear her—"at Fuel Emporium! More like *Low Quality Emporium* if you ask me!"

She laughs hysterically, as if this is a really clever insult. I see the translator bracelet on her wrist and wonder whether it was funnier in whatever language purple people speak. Maybe it rhymed or something.

Fuel! Fuel! Fuel! is a small, cluttered, L-shaped store, with only a single aisle running down the middle and cutting quick to the left. Some of the shelves are stocked—but most are empty and a few are even broken.

"Maybe we should just go straight to Fuel Emporium instead," Becka whispers to me.

"Don't mind the mess," the shopkeeper explains. "It's been a long day."

Except it doesn't really look like "the mess" has anything to do with this particular day.

She turns her head toward the closest shelf.

"Oh dear, that isn't right," she huffs, flipping over a small machine that looks like a Slinky. She puts it back down and the shelf cracks underneath, snapping in two and spilling parts all over the floor. A plume of dust rises into the air, but the woman just brushes the dirt off of her face and keeps talking.

"We're between seasons, you understand. Almost entirely sold out for the trisolar festival. I can barely keep up with demand."

There isn't a single other customer in this store. I peek across the way at Fuel Emporium, which is a lot larger and, compared to Fuel! Fuel! Fuel!, packed with shoppers.

"So what exactly are you looking for?" she asks.

"Fuel for a light speed engine. Enough to travel about 1,500 light years." That should give us enough to get back to Ganymede, return with a rescue party, and then bring everyone home—with a little to spare.

"Of course. Which type of engine, though? Artificial black hole? Wormhole piercer? Gravitation well hyperdrive?"

We stare at her with open mouths. In retrospect (and I'll only ever say this once in my life), we probably should have done a little more homework before coming here. It didn't even occur to me that there were different *types* of light speed engines.

Doesn't mean I wasn't paying attention during my dad's message, though.

"It's an Alcubierre drive?" I try.

She nods. "Inefficient. But they get the job done."

And I know one other thing too: "Our engine runs on quantum hexachloride."

"Doesn't everyone's," she comments. "You stay here and I'll fetch some Alcubierre QHC from my safe."

She steps away from us and rounds the corner at the back of her store. We browse while we wait, even though all the merchandise looks like junkyard trash. The only other things in the shop are a door in the back—now ajar, which must be where she went to access her safe—and a security desk with three screens: One shows the entrance of the shop; another shows the aisle and the desk (I wave my hands and watch myself on the feed); and the third—clearly on the fritz, as it flickers a bit every few seconds—displays a small metal hatch in the corner of a closet-sized room.

At first I figure that the hatch is her safe—it's got a keypad with strange symbols on it. But UNKNOWN NAME comes out after a minute, holding something in her hand, having never once showed up on that third screen. So I guess not.

"Got it," she says, pushing the backroom door shut behind her. She shows us what looks like a ball of tinfoil.

"*That's* quantum hexachloride?" Ari asks.

"Purest blend in the galaxy. That'll be one hundred and fifty-seven Elvidian credits."

I blink at her.

"Okay," UNKNOWN NAME says. "You seem like nice folks. Let's make it a hundred fifty, even."

But all we ever came up with was Ari's "ask nicely" idea.

"We don't have any money," Becka tells her bluntly.

The shopkeeper bursts out laughing. Why do people keep doing that? "Oh you got me! No money. Good one."

We try to explain that we're kids and need help. But she just laughs even harder, muttering as she shoves us out of her store. "Tell your Fuel Emporium bosses they're gonna have to try harder than that!"

"Told you," Becka mutters to us.

I swallow back my disappointment. "Let's try the other place."

We head to the opposite end of the level. Even with the loud cleanup going on around us, I can faintly hear UNKNOWN NAME greeting another happy customer outside her shop: "Go away! Bother those *cheats*"—she really does project her voice pretty impressively—"over at Fuel Emporium instead."

"Now *this* is a store," Ari says.

Fuel Emporium is massive and clean and beautiful—full of neat shelves stocked high with shiny machines. Little flying drones whiz around the store, grabbing items, delivering them to shoppers, and restocking the merchandise. Dozens of aliens (mostly Elvidian) are browsing and buying. There's even an area in the middle where some scientist is demonstrating the power of different types of engines to ooohs and aahhs.

"Welcome to the Fuel Emporium," an Elvidian tells us, opening his arms up wide. "Winner of Fuel Cell Distributor of the Year, every year, since we opened our doors. Proud sponsor of the Galactic Run. I'm Rick."

I share a look with the others. Not the most alieny name we've ever heard.

"How can we serve you?"

I take a deep breath. I don't know why I think this might work better here than in the dingy place across the level.

"We need light speed fuel," I explain. "Quantum hexachloride—"

"Naturally," he mutters.

"—but we don't have any money."

Right on cue: He starts laughing. Another dead end. "Who put you up to this?" Rick asks. "It wasn't that huckster over in Fuel! Fuel! Fuel!, was it? She hasn't done enough today? I'm telling you—can't trust a non-Elvidian for an eighth credit." He gives us a second look. "No offense."

Becka shrugs. "Well, I don't think she trusts you either."

He laughs again. "She doesn't, huh? Because *I'm* the thief around here. Right."

"Please," I beg, changing the subject. "We *need* the fuel for our friends." I look at Becka. "And family. They're in trouble and need our help."

He crouches down to look at us at eye level.

"If you're in trouble, why haven't you called the Minister's office? I'm sure she would be happy to help." He stands back at attention. "Long Live the Minister, of course."

"Of course," Becka copies, saluting. "We love, love, love the Minister, don't we? She's great."

"Love her," I say.

"Wanna marry her!" Ari doubles down.

The guy looks at us strangely as Becka chokes down a laugh.

"Anyway," she continues. "The Minister's office is trying. Really trying. But it's complicated. We *need* fuel. Please—isn't there a job we can do or something? Work for you for a little and earn some fuel?"

The guy looks past us.

"It would take a long time for you to work your way to earning even an ounce of QHC. I don't have any open positions that pay what you—"

He stops.

"That pay what we *what*?" Becka presses.

He's staring out of the store at Fuel! Fuel! Fuel!

"You do seem like nice kids," he says. "Maybe there is a job you can do for me."

"Perfect!" Becka says. Ari and I slap five.

"Follow me," he says in a hush, leading us toward the front of the store.

We stop next to a display window facing the atrium. Inside are maybe eighty or ninety small diamonds, hovering by themselves in rows of ten each, like stars in the corner of an American flag.

"Do you see that?" Rick says.

"See what?" I ask.

"There's one missing," he points. Sure enough, in the second-to-bottom row, near the right side of the window, there's a space where a floating diamond should be.

"What are they?"

"My most valuable possessions. And that thief!"—he yells it out to make sure the Fuel! Fuel! Fuel! lady hears him—"stole it from me. I'm sure of it."

"Why don't you call the police?" Ari asks. "Or the Minister's office."

He sighs. "I've got no proof. It's my word against hers."

And that's when it hits me. My heart thumps and my head buzzes. I can feel my fingers tingling. It's like I've been hit by lightning. I don't know if this how my dad felt when he came up with his idea for the engine, but it has to be close.

The Elvidian grins. "And I want you to steal it back for me."

"But how are we supposed to do that?" Ari asks.

I only half-listen to the rest of the conversation, thinking everything through. The safe. Of course. We break into the safe.

"No clue," Rick is saying. "I tried once—but her safe is impenetrable."

Of course her safe is impenetrable. We don't have to crack it. We need the code.

"You need the code," Rick says like he's reading my mind.

Ha!

"But only she knows it. And she's so paranoid that she probably changes it twice a day."

"Didn't you just say that you tried to break in once?" Becka asks. "Doesn't that make her not paranoid?"

He flicks his ear twice, which must be his species' shorthand for "who cares." "Whatever. She's got a restraining order against me now. Can't go within fifty feet of her store. So if I even set foot in that place . . . well, prison is not an option. Not worth my freedom."

Becka, Ari, and Rick go back and forth for a few more seconds. I look at Becka—I get that she hasn't put it all together yet—but Ari? How has he not figured it out?

"You want fuel?" Rick adds, heading off to a customer. "Break into the safe and bring me my prize. Of course." He shrugs. "If you get caught, I never met you."

He walks away and Ari turns to me in despair.

"How in the world are we supposed to break into an impenetrable safe?"

I grin at him. "We already have."

21

Becka doesn't like being kept in the dark. "You ready to tell us your genius plan?"

"Not yet. Let's wake them up first so I can explain to all of you at once."

We're back on the ship, in the kitchen. And we're standing by the lunch robots with our fingers hovering over their "on" switches.

"Whatever it is," Ari says, "they're not gonna like it."

"Nope," I agree. "Definitely not."

But in our defense, they don't really like anything. When I was in fifth grade, the teachers threw a birthday party for Stingy. But instead of blowing out the candles, Stingy poured motor oil all over the cake. Stingy said it was an accident, but I'm telling you it was on purpose.

"Here we go," Becka announces.

Ari's got Creaky, Becka's got Cranky, and I'm stuck with Stingy. (We played a round of rock-paper-scissors that I lost best-two-out-of-three.) All at once, we push down on the small power buttons on the backs of the robots' necks and the gears inside whir to life.

"Oh my," Creaky says, opening its eyes and immediately stretching out its arms—but one of them falls and hits the floor with a *clang*. These robots are not the realistic, humanish kind of robots. I've seen some of those around on Ganymede—the ones with fake skin and transplanted hair and everything. Sometimes, you can't even tell. These robots are much, *much* older models. They're the boxy, machiney type—soda cans with arms and legs.

"That was a longer assembly than usual," Creaky says, picking up its severed limb and casually screwing it back on. Creaky twists it around a few times and, even though the arm stays put, it still looks a little crooked.

"Yes," Stingy agrees, standing up straight as if cracking its back. "I'm sure Lochner droned on and on."

"I'm still tired," Cranky whines. "Can I just go back to sleep?"

Classic Cranky.

Stingy looks around the kitchen and out toward the cafeteria. "Look at the mess they've made! Who do they expect will clean everything up? Us? Absolutely not. The school year is up for us just as it is for them. They have no respect for free robots. Our ancestors didn't—"

"Whatever," Cranky interrupts. "If anyone asks me to clean, I'm going back into sleep mode."

"I'll have a word with Lochner," Stingy declares, "about the need to show some discipline to these messy, disrespectful—"

"Ahem," I clear my throat.

The three robots spin around and—surprise, surprise—aren't happy to see us.

"Graham, Bowman, Pierce!" Stingy barks like a drill sergeant. "You shouldn't be here. You were supposed to go home for the summer! Did you get lost on the way to the shuttles? And where is the principal with our end-of-the-year paychecks? I have bills to pay."

I try to cut him off. "Listen, Stingy—"

"Not my name."

Oh come on. I know that their nicknames aren't exactly complimentary, but they've earned them fair and square. Besides, their real names are way too hard to remember. "Um, sorry . . . Z-4H7?"

"No!" Cranky whines. "*I'm* Z-4H7!"

"Oh, sorry. Anyway—"

"You don't know my name, Graham?" Stingy asks, clearly offended. "I've been making you food for three years and you don't know my *name*?"

I sigh. We haven't even gotten to the hard part yet. "Z-8I3?"

"Ha," Creaky laughs. "That's *me*!"

Creaky smacks Stingy in the shoulder, which makes a sound like two baking trays clanking against each other. Creaky's arm falls off again. "Ignore it," Creaky says, reattaching it for the second time. "This thing gets worse and worse every year."

"What is my *name*?" Stingy bellows.

One more guess. "Z-9B4?"

"Z-9B4!" Creaky is cracking up now. "Isn't that your second cousin, *Stingy*? The CEO of that shipping company? The one your grandparents are so proud of?"

Stingy roars with rage, which sounds like a clogged garbage disposal.

"A little jealous of a cousin," Creaky whispers in my ear. "Pride of the family. Definitely got all the looks." I'm a little fuzzy on how robot families work—like, how's one robot the grandparent of another?— but now's not really the time to get into that.

"If you cannot remember my name," Stingy says, "then how will you ever succeed in eighth grade?"

"I'll never *get* to eighth grade if you don't let this go! And we have more important things to talk about than whatever name is on your manufacturing certificate!"

"Well, I can't b—"

Becka sticks two fingers in her mouth and whistles like she's hailing a cab from the Andromeda galaxy. "We need your help," she explains to the now-silent room.

"No need to be obnoxious about it," Cranky mumbles.

"What kind of help?" Creaky asks.

I press my hand against the nearest control panel.

"*WELCOME, JACKSONVILLE GRAHAM. OH—I SEE YOU WOKE UP EVERYONE'S FAVORITE ROBOTS.*"

"Because everyone just loves *your* sunny disposition, right?" Creaky says.

"*WELL, IF IT'S A COMPETITION, THEN—*"

"Ship," I interrupt, "not now. Can you just, I don't know, download your logs into their memory banks? So we don't have to catch them up on everything's that's been going on?"

"Ugh," Cranky complains. "Can we not? I really don't feel like interfacing with the ship right now. It's so glitchy."

"*SPEAK FOR YOURSELF. ALSO, I FORGET—WHO WAS IT WHO NEEDED TWO WEEKS OF MAINTENANCE LAST SUMMER?*"

"Logs," Becka insists. "Now."

"*WITH PLEASURE.*"

And for the next few seconds, the robots all make a low ticking noise that I guess is them connecting with the ship's computer. Their eyes spin around and around in their sockets.

Stingy speaks first. "You mean . . ."

"Yep," I confirm.

"And they're . . ."

"Uh huh."

"So we're . . ."

"Exactly."

"What do we do now?" Creaky asks.

That's the question, isn't it? So I explain my plan, from the sea monster store and the kid losing his dragon, to the arcade and the time machine, to the two fuel stores on the level that got hit with what looks like a giant water balloon. When I'm done, Ari looks skeptical.

"So?" I ask him. "What do you think?"

He bites his lip. "It makes sense, I think. But how do you know we can pull it off?"

"Because we already *did*," I explain.

He shakes his head. "No, listen, even if you're right about everything—and I'm not saying you are—it doesn't mean we already did it. It means we already *tried*. Not the same. Because we don't actually know how the story ends."

I take a deep breath. "Well, we won't find out unless we try," I tell him. "You in?"

"I'm in," says Becka firmly. Ari still doesn't look convinced, but he nods anyway. I mean, come on: he was never going to say no to a time travel heist. I turn back to Cranky, Creaky, and Stingy.

"So what do you say? Any volunteers?"

22

"Tokens," the robot says outside the Time Cannon. "Tokens."

Ari hands over the counterfeit coins, which are accepted without a second glance. Ari steps into the boxy machine, straps in, and is quickly replaced by an Elvidian from the near future. Becka goes next—but she hands the tokens to the robot so hard that its arm falls off. Nobody else notices and Becka heads back in time too.

I hand over my fake tokens.

"Evaluating," Creaky says loudly, popping them into an internal compartment. "Evaluating." Creaky drops its voice down to a whisper.

"Maybe I'll actually keep this job," Creaky tells me, the only one of the three to volunteer. But that's all we needed. Like the other robot said earlier: They had open shifts for a token-taker. And the Arcade people gave Creaky the job as soon as the application was transmitted.

"The pay is *bad*," Creaky continues. "But it beats cooking broccoli, I'll tell you that. And I'm not going to have to listen to Cranky and Stingy whine anymore." I smile at its use of our nicknames for them. "It was a toxic work environment, you know? I think this is going to be much better for me."

I'm glad Creaky's feeling so upbeat about sticking its neck out for us. I mean, who knows what the Elvidians do to lawbreaking robots? Send them to AI jail? Take them apart for scrap metal? Turn them permanently offline? Considering the risks, Creaky is being an amazingly good sport.

"Thanks for doing this."

"No problem," Creaky says. "Good luck."

And the former lunch robot sends me exactly six hours into the past, where I join Becka and Ari.

Time travel is actually kind of meh. No twisty clock hallucinations or the feeling of getting sucked down a wormhole or anything fun like that. Just some hissing from a motor, a lot of smoky exhaust steam from a pipe behind my head, and a loud clicking noise. It seems to last a few minutes. I'm totally conscious the whole time—even a little bored. And eventually the door pops back open to basically the same scene that I left behind, minus Creaky as our mole.

"We've got to work fast," I tell the others.

I insisted on the six-hour option, even though Ari wanted to go back two days. I know the exact timeline we need to follow—where we need to be and when. Six hours is the perfect span. I can't predict what happened in the mall before that. And I don't want to take any risks. (Well, aside from the risks of going back in time to steal a diamond from an impenetrable safe. But you get what I mean.)

First stop: outside the sea monster store, where we wait behind a column for the dad and his son to walk out with the baby dragon. When they leave the store, a pretending-to-be-distracted Becka barrels into the kid and knocks the fish bowl from his hands. It shatters to pieces on the ground, splashing water all over them. And she stealthily pockets the tiny animal inside a water-filled plastic bag we brought from the 118.

"Hey, watch out!" the dad shouts, scanning the floor for his lost Strykor.

"Sorry, sorry," Becka mutters, before hurrying away and looping back around toward us. So far, so good.

Second stop: the atrium of the level with the fuel stores, which looks exactly the way I expected—clean, dry, and unharmed. Becka casually drops the Strykor into the full, not-at-all cracked fountain before sneaking off with Ari. They hide behind a pillar near the entrance to Fuel! Fuel! Fuel! while I reach down and toss the little monster some pieces of bread I brought with me from the ship. One minute goes by. Five. Ten. I'm giving him piece after piece, like I'm feeding ducks at a pond. But even after he's nibbled down the entire loaf, nothing happens. Fifteen minutes. Twenty.

When I'm all out, I look over at Ari, who's peeking at me from behind the pillar. I pull my pockets inside out to show him that I'm running on empty. He just shrugs and I can't figure out what I must've missed—until I remember that the bread isn't the only food I've got.

I pull a green and yellow stalk from my back pocket—the free sample we got in the Arcade—and drop the whole half-lettuce/half-corn thing into the fountain. It starts to bubble purple and blue, like the water's suddenly turned to grape soda, as it spills over the sides. I back away from the fountain as quick as I can, but my foot slides out from under me and I fall backwards. I want to move, but I'm frozen, watching the dragon grow to double, triple, fifty times my size.

The fountain cracks in half as the monster spreads its giant flippers and starts flapping over and over, faster and faster. Here's an unexpected freebie: It can fly. Badly.

The monster zips happily around the room, knocking into walls and carving holes into the ceiling. Alien shoppers scatter and scream, crowding near the elevator-cylinders or running to the staircase.

The purple lady in charge of Fuel! Fuel! Fuel! takes the bait and wanders into the atrium to see what's going on. I'm still on the ground and try to get up to hide.

But it's chaos in here and the floor's all slippery and (I guess I knew this would happen, right?) she spots me out of the corner of her eye, crawling away from the fountain.

"Hey you!" she shouts at me, pointing at the creature doing summersaults in the air. "Is that yours? Did you do this?" The dragon nicks the sign above her store. It comes loose at one end and swings downward, sparking as it falls. She looks out at Fuel Emporium, which is essentially unharmed. "Did *they* send you?! Did they?!"

I duck behind a freestanding booth just as a bunch of cleanup robots come running up the steps, along with a few Elvidian soldiers and a rhinogoat wearing a shirt that says "Wrangler" on the back. Together, they catch the Strykor in a giant net and zap it with something that makes it shrink back down to size.

UNKNOWN NAME was only outside of Fuel! Fuel! Fuel! for ten minutes. But it was enough.

"Done," Ari says, huffing and puffing. We've regrouped behind an archway near Fuel Emporium, hopefully out of sight.

He turns on his ring and taps into the tiny camera that he and Becka rigged up while the monster was on the loose. They planted it inside the room with the safe, facing straight at the keypad. Ari projects a holographic image of the keypad against the wall next to us.

"Perfect," I say.

And that's the thing: It doesn't matter that the safe is impenetrable. Because all we need is the *code* to the safe. And it doesn't matter that the shop lady is the only one who knows the code. Because all we need now is for her to type it in. And it doesn't matter that she might change the code twice a day. Because we know exactly when she's going to type it in next and she won't have the chance to change it before we're done.

"Ha!" Becka points. "There we are!"

Sure enough, the three of us—from our past—arrive in the elevators, up from that first trip to the Arcade.

"You again?" UNKNOWN NAME shouts at the pre-time-travel version of me.

"Me?" the other me asks.

"Do I really sound like that?" the *me* me asks Becka and Ari.

It's all getting a little complicated.

We watch as they/we walk into Fuel! Fuel! Fuel! Using the camera we planted, we record the code to the safe when she goes into the back room to get the fuel we had asked for that first time.

"Gotcha," Becka says as Ari replays the code sequence on the wall.

The versions of us from the past—having struck out in Fuel! Fuel! Fuel!—cross the atrium toward Fuel Emporium.

"I'm not gonna lie. I can't believe this is happening," Ari says.

"Well, it's really all thanks to you," I say. "You were right. As usual. Time travel was the way to go."

Ari shrugs, half-embarrassed by the compliment. And I realize he's used to me taking his brilliance for granted. I've really got to change that.

"But what now?" Becka asks. "We don't know the future anymore, right?"

"Well," I explain. "We know one more thing."

I lead them back toward Fuel! Fuel! Fuel! where, again, Ari and Becka sneak off to the side to wait for my diversion.

Right on cue, the purple lady spots me.

"Ugh," she says. "Go away! Bother those cheats over at Fuel Emporium instead."

"But I have some money now," I lie.

Her body language goes from "get lost!" to "get over here!"

"Well why didn't you say so?" She smiles, waving me inside. "Still in the market for some Alcubierre QHC?"

"Actually, I'm going to need a lot more than that."

"Ooh!" she squeals. "Right this way."

I'm able to distract her long enough for Ari and Becka to sneak into the safe room. And when the lady and I round the corner at the back of the aisle—and she peeks at the camera facing the safe—there's nothing. All she sees is the empty room. Or a recording of the empty room at least. Because Ari and Becka did one more thing when they were in here: looped the security feed using a five-second clip of the empty room. Don't ask me how. That's Becka's department. Either way, the safe may be impenetrable, but her camera feed was *not*.

"And what's this?" I ask, pointing to what looks like a glowing milky cube—maybe an inch or two thick—pulsing with the dazzling light of what can only be described as a shrunken star imprisoned in glass.

"Oh." She shrugs, picking up the starbox with her thumb and forefinger, sniffing it, and popping it in her mouth. "Sorry, just my lunch. The day got away from me."

I'm doing my best to keep her occupied but she's getting impatient. Becka and Ari were supposed to get in, type in the code, grab the diamond, and get out. Which means something's wrong.

"Need more time," Becka texts me. "Keep her away from the door."

I get UNKNOWN NAME to turn around as Ari quietly sneaks out of the back room and sprints down the aisle, back into the mall. I panic—but as quickly as Ari leaves (seriously, it couldn't have been more than two seconds), he comes back. With a neat haircut and totally different clothes. This was *not* part of the plan. But whatever he did must've worked, because he tiptoes back into the safe room and slinks out with Becka a minute later.

"Oops!" I say, as Becka and Ari get clear. "Gotta go!"

"But what about your purchase?"

"Next time, thanks!"

I join Ari and Becka by the fountain.

"So?"

Becka opens her hand to reveal the diamond.

"What happened to you?" I ask Ari.

"There was *another* keypad *behind* that keypad," he explains, rolling his eyes.

"So we needed to plant a *second* camera in the past," Becka tells me. "The first one wasn't enough."

"No big deal—" Ari burps. Hard. "'Scuse me. I used the Time Cannon again and took care of it."

I look Ari up and down. "How far back did you go?"

He gives me a mischievous grin.

I shake my head. "What'd you do by yourself for *two days*?"

"Stuff?" is all Ari answers. He blinks innocently, and I know I'm gonna have to get that story out of him later. For now, we walk back to Fuel Emporium and find Rick.

"Back so soon?" he asks.

Becka holds the jewel out to him.

"Ha!" he shouts, snatching it out of her hand. "My trophy!"

"Trophy?" Ari asks.

"Yes! My missing Fuel Cell Distributor of the Year trophy! I knew she took it. I just knew it."

He proudly places it back into the window display.

"I thought it was something valuable," I say.

"Oh, very valuable. To *me*. Sentimentally speaking, of course."

"Whatever," Becka says. "We did the job. Now we need 1,500 light years' worth of Alcubierre QHC."

He nods and smiles wide, particularly after we hear UNKNOWN NAME screech something awful from the other side of the level. She must have opened her safe.

"A deal's a deal."

23

We practically skip out of the mall and back onto the 118.

"Mission accomplished," Becka says, as we enter the main corridor of our ship. "We'll be home in no time."

For once, Ari doesn't get all superstitious on us. He just lets out a triumphant hoot.

We walk back into the cafeteria. It's been cleaned up and the whole place smells like pine and lemony soap.

"The robots?" Ari asks.

"Maybe," I say, as I notice a little handwritten note taped to one of the folding tables: *Cleaned up a little—but don't expect us to make a habit of it. And don't wait for us. We've decided to stay awhile. Sincerely, "Cranky" & "Stingy."*

"You think they're okay?" Ari asks. Guess Creaky isn't going to get that alone time after all.

"They're fine," Becka answers, rolling her eyes. "They hate working here anyway—"

She's cut off by a snapping sound and a quick flash of white light.

"Why are you still here?" an alien asks, his voice raspy and tired. He must have teleported onto our ship. He's dressed in a long dark cloak, hood pulled back revealing his face. He's Elvidian, I think. His red eyes eerily reflect the white walls of the cafeteria. But his skin is deeply lined. As if he's lived too long. Or seen too much. "Unless you want them to capture you—and they *will* capture you, if you stay put much longer."

I stare at the weapon in the visitor's hands, a glance he notices.

"This is not for you, Jack," he says, putting the gun down onto the floor. His voice is familiar—I realize it's the same voice I heard in my head before Orientation. The one that told me it wasn't real.

"How do you know my name?" I ask.

"We don't have much time," is all he says. "I will be called back soon. I've been trying to help you. First, by returning your property to you during your imprisonment." He tilts his head in Ari's direction.

"You mean my Pencil?"

The Elvidian nods. "I had someone slip that device into your cell undetected. I could not risk doing more at the time." He flicks his ear. Maybe I don't understand that gesture after all. "But once you were free, you chose to endanger yourselves further. Though I suppose I should not have been surprised that you ignored my repeated warnings. Just like your father."

"My father?" I say. "You know him?"

"No, but I did try to warn him against building that engine. I tried over and over. But he wouldn't listen. I hoped my messages to you would be more successful."

"Uh, Jack?" Ari asks. "What messages is he talking about?"

I sigh and project the texts up out of my ring: "You must leave." "Leave this place." And more, that I also kept to myself: "They will find you." "They will hunt you down." "The rest of your people are lost. They cannot be helped. Leave them. You can save yourselves now—or save no one if you delay."

"You didn't tell us you've been *getting secret alien text messages* this whole time?" Becka yells.

"What difference did it make?" I yell back. "We needed the QHC. We need to use my dad's engine again. We need to get home and bring back help. What would you have done if I'd told you? Listened to him? Decided to give up? Then what? We'd just fly around this one terrible solar system for the rest of our lives, with the 118ers in jail and our families probably worried sick—all because of my dad? All because of me?"

Becka stares at me and shakes her head. "We wouldn't have given up," she says calmly. "And I can't believe that you thought we would have."

Ari nods. "You should have told us," he says. "We're in this together."

"You voted me the captain," is all I can think to reply.

He rolls his eyes. "So what?"

"Ahem," the Elvidian interrupts. "As I said, little time."

Oh, right. I'd almost forgotten about the alien. "Who are you? Why do you care what happens to us?"

The Elvidian sighs. "My name is Bale Kontra. I will do my best to explain." He throws something into the air: a small, golden sphere that, when it reaches his eye level, explodes into a million pieces.

"Come here," he says, "and watch."

The shards hang in the air for a moment before reassembling themselves into a 3D image. A super-real hologram. We move closer to Bale Kontra as the picture comes together into a familiar scene, floating in the center of the cafeteria like a cloud.

"Is that . . . Jupiter?" Ari asks.

He nods, placing his hands around the sides of the floating diorama and making a gesture like he's pulling clay apart. As he moves his hands farther away from each other, the image zooms out. I circle around the hologram and get my bearings: I can see Io, Europa, Callisto, Ganymede, and lots of Jupiter's other moons too. There are ships everywhere. Other schoolships in orbital rotation, cargo and passenger ships in their space lanes, military and police vehicles on patrol. When I'm standing on one side of the image, I can see through to Mars, Earth, and the Sun. When I move to the other side, I can make out Saturn in the distance. It's as detailed as if it were a portal to the real thing.

"Pay attention," the Elvidian orders, as he swipes a hand across the picture.

It springs to life. The planets and moons begin revolving and ships start moving to and from their destinations. He grabs the outside of it again and tilts it seventy or eighty degrees, like he's turning a globe. Next he squeezes his palms together, zooming in on a small speck toward the outer orbit of Ganymede.

"That's us," I realize.

"Yes," he says, zooming out just a bit so we have a better view.

He waves an arm at the hologram and sets the display on fast-forward. The 118 orbits a spinning Ganymede, day after day after day. Sunrise, sunset, sunrise, sunset. A time-lapse video of space.

"I told him," the Elvidian explains, as the weeks march on inside the cloud, "that if he was discovered, consequences would ensue. But he wouldn't listen. And I couldn't explain fully, in case someone was listening in. There were only so many messages I could send undetected. Eventually, it became too dangerous and I had to cut off the connection."

"But what were you trying to warn him about?" Becka asks.

"This," he says. "The Quarantine." Suddenly, another ship materializes next to the 118, blotting out the view of Ganymede behind it. It's enormous, and its black hull shimmers like it's made of a pool of translucent ink. The

Elvidian waves his arm the other way and the scene slows again. It's back to replaying the recording in real time.

"That's what attacked us?" I ask.

He nods and continues: "I will make this as simple as I can: The Minister is the ruler of our system. But that is not all she controls. She is extremely powerful, and she has extremely powerful allies. Think of them as a committee."

As he's speaking, the alien vessel passes directly in front of Jupiter. Against the background of that massive and colorful planet, we can make out the ship's silhouette more clearly—like a giant sea urchin, with sharp black tentacles reaching out in every direction. A miniature, flying version of Elvid IV. Suddenly, the vessel glows brightly for a moment, flooding space with light that explodes outward like a shockwave in every direction. When the light hits the 118, it tumbles away from Ganymede, out of control.

"The dark matter required to prime the Quarantine is too unstable to release in a single moment. When the Quarantine vessel arrives, it disperses an initial shockwave to commence the process and then—over a period of several minutes—floods the target area with energy sufficient for its purpose."

I only understand a little of that, but enough to know the only question that really matters: "And what *is* its purpose?"

"Think of the Quarantine as a security system of

sorts," he answers, "designed and operated by a secret committee of system leaders. Its purpose is to make sure the galaxy remains a peaceful place."

Becka raises an eyebrow.

"At least, that's what the committee claims. The members pretend that it's about keeping us safe—when in reality, it's about keeping themselves in power. Preventing new races from joining the galactic community. Maintaining the status quo."

"Not sure I'm following," Becka says.

"The committee has spies everywhere, monitoring not just our League of Independent Systems but also the primitive races like yours. There has not been an awakening for many years. Not because there are no young species left. But because when the committee discovers that a primitive race is close to developing the technology needed to travel the stars, they use the Quarantine to prevent the awakening from taking place."

We hear a faint echo of a voice coming from inside the image: "**QUARANTINE IN FIVE MINUTES.**"

"You know the rest," the Elvidian says, as he fast-forwards the scene again. We watch as the 118 hurtles helplessly away from Ganymede and listen as the familiar robotic voice counts down.

"But not really," I point out. "We activated the light speed engine before the Quarantine actually kicked in. What would've happened if we'd stuck around?"

Bale Kontra gestures at the hologram. "What you

are looking at is the most powerful teleportation device ever created. It grabs hold of the supposed threat and sends it to a far-off star system that functions as the committee's dumping ground."

"And where's that?" asks Ari.

He shakes his head. "I have no idea. The Quarantine is a closely guarded secret. It took me many years to even learn of its existence. Many details are still unknown to me."

I think about how my dad was down on Ganymede. If the Quarantine was going after the "threat," it might have been targeting more than the 118 and its light speed engine. It could've also been targeting my dad—the guy who *made* the light speed engine. Which would mean . . .

The countdown concludes: "**THREE. TWO. ONE.**" And we watch as the 118 vanishes into nothingness and darkness blots out the whole projection.

"Can you rewind a few seconds?" I ask the Elvidian. "Rewind and zoom out, and slow it down a little?" My voice comes out kind of strangled. I'm hope my hunch is wrong, but—

The image zooms out and the scene reverses, back to before we jumped away. He plays it again, more slowly. And I watch as, milliseconds after the 118 disappears, the darkness fills the space where it once was, plus *all the space around it*, blanketing Ganymede—its atmosphere, its surface, everything—with its energy.

"Did the Quarantine target *everyone* on Ganymede?" I whisper. That sounds impossible—but that word just doesn't mean as much as it used to.

"I'm afraid," says Bale Kontra, "you were the only ones to escape."

The light fades. And the image dissolves into dust that congeals back into the golden sphere, which falls back into the alien's open palm.

The three of us are staring at him in stunned silence. My dad, Ari's and Becka's parents, the population of our whole moon, has been kidnapped by aliens and sent to a mystery location that could be literally anywhere in the galaxy.

"This is why I contacted you," Bale Kontra tells me. "I saw that you were risking everything to get more fuel, to use your light speed engine again. To get back to your moon, presumably. But you will only be returning to an abandoned homeworld, where the Minister will easily find you again. You should instead find a remote place to stay hidden. Please."

"How do you know all this?" Becka demands. "And why do you care what happens to us?"

"I oppose the agenda of that corrupt committee." Which doesn't really answer her questions. "I believe that the galaxy would be a better place with the new races in it, not worse. But I am no match for the Minister."

He's about to say more, but he's interrupted by a

short, shrill siren coming out of his translator bracelet. "I have to leave," he tells us.

Ari grabs his arm. "But . . ." He pauses, clearly trying to think of the most important question of all the questions we still have. ". . . what do we do now?"

Bale Kontra effortlessly pulls his arm out of Ari's grip and picks up his gun. Then he touches his wrist cuff and vanishes into thin air, leaving behind only a single word.

"Run."

24

"Let's get off this planet," I say.

"And then what?" Ari still looks frantic. "If we can't go back to Ganymede . . ."

My hands tighten around the lump of QHC I'm holding. "Earth," I say. "We'll go to Earth instead."

It's our best bet at this point. Our only bet.

"Get to the bridge," I tell Ari and Becka. "I'll be there in a few minutes."

Becka opens her mouth like she has something to add, but there's no time to get sidetracked.

"Go!" I yell at them. I dash off toward the engine room with the QHC clenched in my fist. Hopefully, by the time Ari gets us in orbit and far enough away from the surface, I've figured out where this thing goes.

I wind my way back to the glass observation deck. There are a few auxiliary lights beaming a low glow all around me, but with the engines off, the room is still pretty dark. Creepy.

With everything that's happened, this place makes me feel weird—all jumbled up inside. I'm angry at my dad for putting us at risk, especially after he was warned. But I'm also proud of him for making something great and important. I feel special that he shared it with me. That he named it after me. But I also feel guilty that I ever used it.

Then again, if I hadn't, we'd be who-knows-where, trapped with the rest of Ganymede's lost population. No one would be able to tell the rest of our solar system about what's out here. About what happened.

I press my hand against the cool glass walls.

"WELCOME, JACKSONVILLE GRAHAM."

"I've got more light speed fuel," I tell the ship, holding the silver ball out in front of me. "Any idea where it goes?"

As I ask this question, the regular engines activate. Ari must be taking us up. I watch as the giant pistons on the inside of the larger boxy chamber—the one that surrounds the glass observation deck—start moving faster and faster. The ship jolts around as Ari tries to get his bearings.

And maybe because it gets how much danger we're in, the ship just says: *"YES."*

"Great. Show me."

I hear a rumble from somewhere along one of the outer walls of the engine room, and a walkway extends out toward me. It's wide at the far end and narrows as it gets closer. When the edge of the path touches up against the glass, a panel—big enough for person to walk through—slides open next to me. I'm hit with a gust of hot wind and an earsplitting blast of loud noise. One of the large pistons is still broken and scraping against a nearby wall. Scrape, scrape, scrape.

I walk out onto the hovering path.

The massive moving parts of the engine are shooting air around the room. I take a few steps onto the narrow walkway. *Scrape, scrape, scrape.* It feels like I'm tightrope-walking across a windy canyon. *Keep it together, Jack. You can do this.* There's a cracked pipe somewhere above me that's spraying water down onto my head. I look up and then back down at the floor fifty feet below me—which makes me dizzy.

Ari dips us down and back up again. *Scrape, scrape, scrape.* It's hard to keep perspective in here. I don't think that the light speed engine was meant to be refueled mid-flight. I should have had him wait. Maybe that's what Becka wanted to tell me. I really need to start listening better.

I try to take a few more steps but lose my footing and stumble forward onto my knees. I'm at least able to grab the sides of the platform to steady myself so I don't fall off.

There's no time for this. If it's too hard to walk, fine. I decide to crawl the rest of the way, clutching the edges of the path until I reach the other side.

I'm finally up against the wall, kneeling next to a

small metallic panel. It blends in so well with the surface around it that—unless you know what you're looking for—it can't be seen.

He was right here. Exactly where I am right now.

I place my hand against an access screen.

"WELCOME, JACKSONVILLE GRAHAM."

And the panel slides open, revealing a small cubby, no larger than a kitchen drawer. It's empty and smooth, except for an inch-deep groove in the bottom and some silver flecks that I guess are left over from the expended QHC. I look down at my hand, still holding the chunk of fuel, and back over at the slit in the panel. It looks to be the perfect size. So I lift my arm and put the rock into its place.

At first, nothing happens. But after a moment, the QHC begins to pulse, faster and faster. Soon it's way too bright for me to even look at and I'm worried that I've done something wrong. That I accidentally *engaged* the light speed engine before we've broken orbit. According to the map we got from the Minister, Elvid IX has light speed jamming too.

Do I take it out? Is it dangerous? Can I even touch it anymore? A wire automatically unfurls from somewhere inside the glowing rock. It pierces the circuitry surrounding the panel and the pulsing slows to a clock-like rhythm.

"INSTALLATION COMPLETE," the ship tells me. *"THE GANYMEDE IS ONCE AGAIN CAPABLE OF FASTER-THAN-LIGHT TRAVEL."*

The Ganymede. I had forgotten about that.

"Thanks," I tell the ship. "So you like your new name?"

"*MEH, IT'S OKAY,*" the ship answers. "*RECHARGE COMMENCING. IT'LL BE ABOUT HALF AN HOUR.*"

"Got it," I say. "Thanks, Ship."

***

I join Ari and Becka on the bridge. They're sitting by their posts, and I retake my own seat in the center of the room. In front of me, through the window, I can see the colorful rings of Elvid IX and the endless coat of ships moving around the busy planet.

"Hey," I say. "The light speed engine will be ready to go in half an hour."

"We wanted to talk to you about that, Jack," Ari says.

Uh oh. Whenever Ari tacks my name on to the end of a sentence, it means something's wrong: "No, the quantum thermodynamics test is *today*, Jack." "Principal Lochner's yelling at your dad out in the hallway, Jack." "I think I ate a bad taco, Jack."

"Just hear me out," he says, looking to Becka for support. She nods and he continues. "I don't think we should go to Earth. Not yet, anyway."

"What?" I ask. "Why not?"

"You heard Bale whats-his-name," says Ari. "The Minister will find us again if we go back."

"But we're not going to Ganymede."

"I know. But what if we get to Earth and she just comes after us there?"

I sigh, looking impatiently from Ari to Becka. "We might get caught by the Minister no matter what we do. But what's the alternative?"

"The alternative," says Becka, "is that we try to save the other 118ers ourselves, before we go to Earth. That way, even if the Minister comes after us, we'll all be together."

I look from Ari to Becka and back again. Do they seriously think that this is a good idea?

"No way," I tell him. "We've talked about this already. They know that we escaped. Elvid IV is probably crawling with traps or security or whatever—there are a million reasons why we shouldn't do this alone."

"But we're *not* alone," Becka says. "Think about what the three of us have been able to do."

I see Ari smile and I worry that Becka is clouding his judgment.

"If we got shot out of the sky above Elvid IV," I say, "we won't be helping *anyone*. At least if we get to Earth, we can tell everyone what's happened. Our government has scientists and the military and all kinds of experts. They'll be able to protect us and come up with a real plan."

"Assuming we actually manage to talk to someone in the government," Becka says. "And what makes you think they'll pay attention to us? What if they're too distracted dealing with the Quarantine to try to help save a few stupid kids and teachers? Or what if—they listen to our story, believe us, and then decide helping us isn't worth the risk?"

"Look," says Ari, "we've got the QHC. We can use it any time we want. So if our rescue attempt doesn't work, we can head to Earth *then*."

"Not if the rescue attempt ends with us getting captured or worse!"

"Diana is there," Becka reminds me. "I'm not abandoning my sister. I just can't."

"No one is saying you should. But if we try to do this ourselves and fail, no one will come for any of us. Nobody back home will have any way of figuring out where we are or how to reach us. You, me, and Ari—your sister, all of us—we'll all be stuck here. Cut off."

Becka stands up. "But what if we go to Earth and never see anyone in that prison again? That's a hundred people we should have at least *tried* to save. If we leave them, then I'll—" She pauses abruptly, correcting herself. "Then we'll really be alone."

I get it. I do. If I had a sister, I'd probably feel the same way.

But she isn't thinking straight. We're in over our heads. And I don't want to risk being the one who ruins everything. Again. The one who makes a mistake that gets us thrown in jail. Again.

The one who gets us stuck out here forever.

This story already begins with a Graham making a mistake. I can't let the story end that way too.

But I'm not going to be able to change Becka's mind. I know that. And there's no way she's changing mine. I look at Ari, who's no help at all.

"I'm the captain," I say. "So I choose."

Becka rolls her eyes. "Oh, get real. You're *not* the captain. You're just sitting in someone else's chair." She glances over at Ari. "Besides, *we* already decided. We took a vote without you."

I look at Ari again, who's refusing to look back at me.

This is ridiculous. I'm right and I know it. And I bet Ari knows it too. But he likes her and doesn't want her to hate him. And she probably *would* hate him if he sided with me and we left Diana on Elvid IV.

"Ari, don't be stupid. You don't have to only do whatever Becka wants just because you're in love with her."

Oh no.

My mouth finishes that last sentence about half a second before my brain catches up and realizes what it's doing. I don't even need to see Ari's face to know that I've gone too far.

"I'm sorr—I didn't mean to—"

"No," he says, staring right at me. He's breathing slowly and angrily, like he's trying to stop himself from

219

hyperventilating. I've never seen him (the *real* him, anyway) this upset.

"This has nothing to do with—" He looks over at Becka and gulps loudly. "With that. You're just wrong. And she's just right. Period. Of course it's risky. But I'd rather try and fail than spend the rest of my life wondering if there's something else we could have done. If we leave the 118ers behind, that'll be on us. The Quarantine sent away everyone on Ganymede. You willing to lose even more?"

I don't know what to say. I think about my dad—wherever he is now—and about what *he* would do. What risks *he* would take. And decide I should probably do the opposite.

I shake my head. Even taking the time to *think* about attempting a rescue is stupid. I'm the only one with real control over this ship and I'm going to use it before we get ourselves killed.

I spin my chair around so that I'm facing away from them, looking at the window.

"No," I say. "I'm sorry. We're not going back. I'm still the only one who has full access to this ship's systems. And I can take away your access any time I want. So we're going to do this *my* way. The vote doesn't matter."

They say nothing. I can feel Becka's glare boring a hole into the back of my head and Ari's disappointment melting a hole into the floor beneath his feet.

"Computer, engage Protocol 061999."

"LIGHT SPEED ENGINE REQUIRES SEVEN-TEEN ADDITIONAL MINUTES TO RECHARGE."

"Fine." I stand up. "Just let me know when we're ready, okay?"

"SURE," it says. *"BUT YOU'RE STILL A JERK."*

"Ugh."

I need to get off this bridge for a while. This is the right decision. I know it is. But if I have to sit here for the next seventeen minutes I'm going to implode.

"Keep us in orbit," I tell Ari, standing up and heading for the door. "As soon as we're beyond the jamming—as soon as we can use the light speed engine—we're going home."

I know that he's mad at me. I can't blame him. But I'm hoping that he'll still use his "Aye, aye, Captain" salute. Show me that we'll be okay, in spite of this fight. But he doesn't say anything. Instead, he just looks down at his screen, powers up the regular engines, and aims us a little farther away from the giant planet behind us.

25

"Here, Doctor Shrew! Here boy!"

You know how time flies when you're having fun? Well, I don't know anything about that. But the opposite is definitely true. When you're really *not* having fun— for example, if you just possibly ruined your best friendship and almost everyone else you know is imprisoned in alien jail *and* YOU ARE STILL IN SCHOOL—then time does not fly. It crawls like an injured snail in a coma trying to climb up a down escalator.

I need to make it up to Ari. Show him that I'm sorry. That I still have his back. Which is why—while I wait for the engine to recharge—I'm in the kitchen, calling his hamster's name, holding a stalk of celery I found in the main fridge.

The celery is a little rotten and droops in my hand like it's as miserable as I am.

"Here, boy!"

Whistle, whistle, whistle.

"Here, Doctor Shrew!"

Whistle, whistle, whistle.

Even though we put him back in his cage after his performance as Shrew, Prince of Darkness, he was missing again when I checked a minute ago. According to the ship's life sign scanner, he's somewhere in the kitchen. I open all the drawers. Inspect the fridges and the ovens. And I peek inside unsealed containers of food. But no luck. I chuck the celery against one of the walls in frustration. It's not very dramatic. The celery stalk doesn't shatter to pieces or even bounce off the wall—instead, it just sticks to the digital paper like a wet strand of spaghetti and slides *slllloooouunmmwllllyyyyyy* down to the floor.

I start to panic. What if they're right? What if—even in the best-case scenario—we manage to get back to Earth and still can't help anyone?

"*Squeak!*"

My ears perk up. I spin around in place like a top, scanning the floor.

"*Squeak!*"

Like a knight in shining fur, Doctor Shrew comes nnuttling toward me. I have no idea where he's been hiding this whole time. He sprints toward the celery that's slumped over on the floor. I don't think he even notices when I bend down and scoop him up. He just keeps running his legs in midair like he's on an invisible treadmill.

"Relax, Doc. It's me."

I drop a still-panicking Doctor Shrew down into his cage. He's too crazed to notice and, with his legs still moving, he face-plants into one of the cage's clear plastic sides. It takes him more head bumps than it should to figure out that he's stuck.

I click the top of the cage into place with this paper-clip-and-Velcro lid lock I made so he'll stop escaping every five minutes. Something to show Ari that I really care, you know?

Speaking of Ari, his voice booms from the loud-speaker: "It's almost time. Better get up here."

I feel good about this. Doctor Shrew is one of Ari's favorite things in the whole universe. Ari will be so glad to see him, so happy that I found him, so impressed by the cage's next-gen safety features, that he'll definitely forgive me. I leave the cafeteria with a spring in my step and follow the hallway back down toward the bridge. The doors slide open in front of me and I walk in.

"Hey guys," I say, trying to act like everything's fine. "Here," I turn to Ari, placing Doctor Shrew's cage down next to his computer console. "I found him wandering around."

Ari barely reacts at all.

"Thanks," is all he says.

And it stings.

"Sure," I respond, clearing my throat. I walk away from him and retake my chair in the middle of the bridge, trying to shake off my hurt feelings. Whatever. It's fine. "You're welcome."

I look out of the window in front of me. I wanted to try and fix things with Ari sooner rather than later. I didn't want us to have to face whatever's ahead while we're in a fight. But I don't have a choice.

"*THE LIGHT SPEED ENGINE IS NOW FULLY RECHARGED*," the ship says. "*AND YOU ARE STILL A JERK*."

"Thanks."

I press my hand against one of the small computer consoles on the armrest of the captain's chair. Time to go.

"*WELCOME, JACKSONVILLE GRAHAM*."

"Ship, set a course for Earth. As close as you can get. Engage Protocol 061999 when ready."

There's a pause, like it's thinking things over. Maybe the engine wasn't done recharging after all?

"*ACCESS DENIED*."

"What?" That doesn't make sense. "Ship," I say again firmly, sitting back in my chair. It must have been some kind of glitch. "This is Jacksonville Graham. Set a course for Earth. Engage Protocol 061999."

"*ACCESS DENIED*."

"Access denied?! How? By who?!"

This time, the computer doesn't miss a beat. "*BECK-ENHAM PIERCE*," it answers. I think I hear a note of satisfaction in its voice. "*AND ARIZONA BOWMAN*."

No.

My heart plummets through the floor. I spin around and stare back at them. Becka is meeting my eyes, but Ari is looking down at Doctor Shrew.

"Ari figured out how to overwrite the control software," Becka tells me. "The ship helped a little too. We removed your access when you left the bridge."

I stand up and storm over to Ari, my blood boiling. He's still looking down at Doctor Shrew. "How *could* you? That was my dad's software you overwrote. *He* was the one who gave me access. You had no right to take it away."

He looks me straight in the eyes, not the least bit guilty. "No," he says. "We're supposed to be a team. We're supposed to make decisions together. But instead, you've been mean. And bossy. You think everyone else's judgment is getting clouded by their feelings. Becka's because of Diana. Mine because of . . ." He clears his throat. ". . . stuff. But you have it backwards. *You're* the one who's not thinking straight. Not us."

I can't believe this. It's taking all my willpower not to explode. I clench my teeth and look back at Becka.

She stands up and walks around her console toward me, cracking her knuckles like she's on the attack. I don't care. I'm not moving. I plant my feet.

But she doesn't punch me. Instead, she walks past me toward the center of the bridge and takes a seat in *my* chair.

Say whatever you want about me never having actually been in charge of anything. Say that all I've ever been was a kid playing pretend. But that chair is real. This ship is real. I *am* the captain.

Or, at least, I *was* the captain.

Until my crew staged a mutiny.

26

I sit down in Becka's boring, non-captainy chair, in front of her former computer station. She's sitting happily where I used to sit, spinning round and round in the chair, like it's the teacup ride on Walt Disney Moon.

I never should have given them access to the computer. I never should've trusted them.

And I hope you don't mind, but I'm gonna speed through this next part. It doesn't really involve *me* all that much anyway. (So it can't be that good of a story.)

Anyway, Ari and Becka's brilliant plan is this: (1) Rebroadcast the code that the Elvidian guard gave us—the one that got us off Elvid IV in the first place. (2) Dress Becka up in the helmet that the guard left behind, along with one of Ari's old Halloween costumes. (3) Send a message to the prison saying that the Minister is ordering the release of all the umjerrylochners. (4) Pick everyone up from the roof. (5) Go home.

"And we have a fail-safe," Ari says way too many

times to be reassuring. "The second there's trouble, we use the light speed engine to get out of here."

This is obviously the worst plan I've ever heard. There are a thousand reasons why it shouldn't work. For example: #1: Wouldn't the guard who gave us the code have already reported it stolen? #18: Why would the Elvidians believe that the Minister gave us orders? #613: How are we supposed to get far enough away from the planet to use the light speed engine if (or when) something goes wrong?

But it works.

Breaking everyone out of jail is unbelievably easy. Without any help from me, Becka and Ari successfully pull off steps 1–4.

They've "assigned" me to head down to the hangar bay and bring everyone up to speed. The 118ers are all onboard now, and the hangar bay doors close behind them.

"What's happening?" Principal Lochner asks me.

"Do you want the good news or the bad news?"

"Let's start with the bad news." The teachers and crewmembers gather next to him as the students mill around in confusion.

"Okay," I say, but my voice is drowned out by everyone's worried chatter. I hop on top of a small metal storage box. "Okay!" I shout, getting everyone's attention. The room quiets down. "Hi. We don't have a lot of time. So here are the highlights. Becka, Ari, and I stole back our ship and got our light speed engine refueled. We're trying to get home. Back to Earth, actually. Ganymede is, um—" I think twice about telling the total truth here. We can explain everything later. "Ganymede might be dangerous."

"Our light speed engine?" is all Principal Lochner asks.

Mrs. Watts glares at me like she wishes I'd left her in jail.

"Long story," I explain. "And I'll tell you everything once we're safe. I promise. For now, all you need to know is that things might go bad really fast. If you ask me, there's no way the Elvidians won't come after us. And we can't use the engine to get back to our solar system until we're far enough away from the planet. Oh yeah, and there's a giant alien conspiracy to keep younger civilizations from ever achieving high tech capabilities."

Mr. Cardegna just blinks.

"Wasn't there good news?" Ms. Needle asks after a few seconds.

"No one's blown us up yet?" I offer. "And we're all together now? Oh, and time travel's a thing. So there's that."

Principal Lochner nods. "Jack is right. We're together now, and we're back on the 118." He turns to the three members of the ship's crew. "Harriet, Georgia, Tim, get us out of here."

The crewmembers don't look too excited to be back in action, but Harriet goes over to the nearest control panel anyway and puts her hand on it.

"*WELCOME, LAKE HARRIET LITTLE*," the ship says. "*YOUR ACCESS HAS BEEN REVOKED.*"

Harriet stares blankly at the control panel. Principal Lochner turns to me. "What's going on?"

"I think Ari and Becka locked everyone else out," I say.

The ship rocks to one side—nothing bad, just Ari's usual bumpy takeoff. "So who's flying the ship?" demands Principal Lochner.

"Uh, Ari."

His eyes go supernova and I think fast about my options. Ari and Becka locked me out too, and I haven't gotten over that. It would be easy to work with Principal Lochner and get the adults back in control.

But—no thanks to me—Ari and Becka's plan is really working. Now's not the time to get in the way.

Besides, we started all this. We should be the ones who finish it.

"Don't worry," I say. "We've got this. Becka's on scanning and I'm in charge of the light speed engine." A bit of a lie, but whatever. "So the rest of you can just, uh, hang out until we get home."

Principal Lochner looks at me skeptically.

"They're *children*," Mrs. Watts reminds him, as if I'm not standing a foot away from her. It's like the first thing I've heard her say since the assembly. "They all need to be disciplined."

Principal Lochner doesn't look at her. "Later, Enid. Later." He's still staring me down, wrestling with what to do. Finally, he speaks. "All right. I can see that it's going to take a while for us to understand everything that's happening. So in the meantime, I guess I have no choice but to trust your judgment, Jack." He turns to the teachers. "Take everyone to the gym and stay there until this is all over. It's the safest place on the ship—farthest away from the outer hull in case something happens."

He looks over at Ms. Needle.

"The hooks in the floor? By the bleachers? Grab the extra-long bungee straps. Jump ropes. Whatever. Strap everyone in as best you can."

She nods, and Principal Lochner turns to Harriet.

"Go with everyone to the gym," he says.

"Oh *thank you*," she exhales, which isn't that surprising, I guess. The crew isn't known for their work ethic.

He looks at her sternly. "And be ready with a remote flight portal just in case."

She nods sheepishly. "Of course, boss."

Principal Lochner turns back to me.

"But if you think that *I* am not going to come with you to *my* command bridge—well, that's not going to happen." He extends an arm toward the corridor behind the shuttles. "After you."

***

We rejoin Ari and Becka on the bridge just in time for everything to go wrong.

I sit back down behind Becka's old computer console and Principal Lochner silently joins me. He pulls a small bench out from under the controls, sits down, and straps himself in with a seatbelt I didn't see before.

"Don't you think you all should be wearing your seatbelts?" he asks.

Becka turns around to give him the stink-eye. But I can see it dawning on her that, yeah, we probably *should* be wearing our seatbelts. We all strap in.

"Almost there, Jack," Becka says smugly. "Look out for an 'I told you so.'"

But as we break low-orbit—still a few minutes away from the edge of the light speed jamming—the screen in front of us flickers with static.

We keep moving, because what else are we supposed to do? But the static slowly clears and reveals a familiar image: an Elvidian woman, holding a scepter made of lasers, sitting on a black crystal throne.

"Hello," she says. "I am the Minister."

Becka immediately slumps down into her seat as Principal Lochner asks, "Was that supposed to happen?" And I'm sorry, I know this is a bad time, but I can't help it. I lean forward as far as I can stretch and whisper in Becka's ear.

"I told you so."

27

"You've traveled so far and now have nothing to say?"

What's there to say? We've been caught. The flash of satisfaction I felt at Becka's expense disappears. It doesn't matter who was right and who was wrong. We're all going down now.

But Becka quickly finds her nerve. "Oh please," she says. "You're not so tough. We managed to escape your prison *and* get back here *and* rescue everyone else."

"*Almost* rescue," the Minister clarifies. "And let me tell you a different story, shall I? A story of a primitive ship manned by three children and of an escape that was *permitted* to happen. Up to a point."

And I'm listening to them. I am. But mostly, I'm staring at the screen, at the Minister, at what's *behind* the Minister. Eight or ten other Elvidians standing in a semi-circle around her. Some kind of council? Military leaders? They're dressed in these dark cloaks, with hoods pulled almost entirely over their eyes, so I can barely tell them apart. Except for one of them. Standing at the Minister's right shoulder. Creases running down his cheeks. Eyes exposed. Looking right at me.

"I will confess," the Minister goes on, "I had not anticipated your initial jailbreak. I still do not quite understand how you managed to convince the guard of your fabricated illness. But no matter. I quickly recognized it as an opportunity."

The Elvidian behind the Minister—the one making eyes at me—lets his hood slip even further, which confirms it: Bale Kontra. The Elvidian who's been helping us. He's here. With *her*

I share a quick look with Ari and Becka. They've both noticed too.

Which is when Bale Kontra lets his eyes go wide for just a moment, as if to tell us, *Don't say a word.* And maybe also, *Why would you come back here after all my warnings?*

"You see," the Minister continues. "I distrusted you humans from the start. First your little ship has the nerve to think it can travel the stars. Then you evaded the Quarantine and entered Elvidian space, which gave you certain"—she says this last word like it tastes like too much garlic—"rights."

"I knew you were trouble. Unworthy. But we are a law-abiding people. And you had only managed to break one law: unauthorized parking. In order to assume jurisdiction over you and get rid of you permanently, I needed to wait for you to commit a more serious crime. Escaping from custody and staging a prison break will do nicely."

I knew it was too easy.

"I assumed you would return for your fellow prisoners eventually. And here you are! In the wake of *this* violation, I can convince the others that the Quarantine is warranted again—to send you all away for good."

I feel sick. We walked right into the Minister's trap. And it was all for nothing.

I try to send a telepathic message through space and into Bale Kontra's mind. (Hey, nothing's impossible anymore, right?) *Help us! Do something!* But he doesn't react. I can't really blame him. He warned us, and we didn't listen.

"Now," the Minister concludes, "I'm afraid that your little adventure is over. Shut down your engines and wait. One of our tow ships will be along to link with your vessel in exactly eleven minutes. It will bring you to a secure location from which you will await the Quarantine." When she says that last word, a chill runs down my spine. I wonder why she doesn't just Quarantine us on the spot, but I remember what Bale Kontra said about the Minister's committee being "secret." I guess even her fellow Elvidians would think she's off her rocket if they knew what she's been up to.

The screen shuts off and we're left with the view of the three suns and a tiny speck rising from the surface of the planet: the tow ship, heading toward us. I look over at Becka and regret my "I told you so." We were *all* wrong. (Some more than others, but who's counting?) She's frozen, staring ahead out the window.

"So I assume that wasn't part of the plan," Principal Lochner says.

"Becka?" I ask, ignoring the principal for a second. "You okay?"

I stand up and she turns around to face me, wiping her cheeks with her palms.

"I—I thought we could help," she says.

"I know." I'm not mad at her anymore. How could I be? She was just trying to do the right thing.

She looks right at me, blinking hard to ward off any more tears. "I'm sorry."

"Me too." I take a deep breath. "But we're still a team. And we can still get out of this. Together."

She nods and presses her hand down onto one of the screens on the captain's chair.

"*WELCOME, BECKENHAM PIERCE.*"

"Ship, give light speed access back to Jacksonville Graham."

"*ACCESS RESTORED,*" the ship says. "*BUT I DON'T THINK I'M GOING TO CALL HIM CAPTAIN, IF IT'S ALL THE SAME TO YOU.*"

Principal Lochner raises an eyebrow and just asks, "Captain?"

Becka sighs, gets up from the leather chair, and nudges me away from her old station, her eyes puffy and red. "You can take all computer access away from me if you want," she offers. "Totally shut me out of the system. I'd understand."

It's tempting. I mean, this is Becka: The girl who mercilessly humiliated me just a few hours ago. But she's also the girl who turned our cafeteria's digital paper into an epic diversion. The girl who pulled a stun gun on our alien prison guard. The girl who came charging back here to rescue everyone. I haven't agreed with everything she's done. But without her, we never would've made it this far.

It's us against the galaxy. We need each other.

"No," I say. "You keep computer access. But thanks. And you know what? The ship's right."

"*ALWAYS*," it interjects.

"I'm not the captain," I clarify. "From here on out—for however long we're on this ship, anyway—let's all take turns sitting in this seat. Deal?"

I extend a hand.

"Deal," she agrees, shaking it.

Ari grins at me.

I take a deep breath, sit back down in the captain's seat (for now), and think.

The Minister told us to stay put. But do we really have to listen? I don't see any other ships out here. We can still make it. I mean, she doesn't know everything, right? She told us herself: She didn't expect us to get off Elvid IV in the first place. Which means she can't see what happens inside our ship—so maybe she doesn't know that we refueled the light speed engine.

If she still thinks we're running on empty—

"Ari?" I ask. "Are we far enough away to use the light speed engine?"

He looks down at his console. "I don't think so. We're probably one or two minutes out still."

"Becka?" I ask. "Any ships out there?"

"No." Her voice is steadier—the confidence is coming back. "Nothing. It's all clear."

Almost there.

"Ari, take us straight out and away. Let me know the second we're far enough from the planet."

"Aye, aye," he says.

The ship rumbles and we begin to move away from Elvid IV. The Minister can give whatever orders she wants, but she can't shoot us down with her laser-red eyes alone. The tow ship is still ten minutes away, out of range, and there's nothing else around. By the time even one ship blasts off from the surface of the planet and gets within firing range, we'll be long gone.

As expected, our screen gets hijacked again.

"I believe I instructed you to stay put."

"We just wanted to get one last look at your solar system before the Quarantine," I tell her. "It's just *so* beautiful."

Behind her, Bale Kontra gives the tiniest shake of his head.

I ignore him. If he doesn't want to help us anymore, we're going to have to help ourselves.

The Minister eyes me suspiciously. "Shut down your engines and await the tow ship or I'll give the order to have your ship destroyed. It will be an easy order to give, believe me."

"Oh yeah?" Becka says, and she doesn't sound shaken anymore. She's back to being the T-Bex we all know and fear. "What'll you shoot us with? There's nothing out here."

"Becka," Principal Lochner warns quietly. He's right. We don't need to egg her on.

"Nothing out here," the Minister echoes, flashing a toothy, yellow smile. "Ah, of course. How silly of me."

The Minister leans backward and turns her head to the side, speaking directly to Bale Kontra. "Tell the defense squadrons to suspend cloaking."

Bale Kontra leans forward and whispers a question into her ear, staring directly at me as he speaks.

"Yes," she answers, turning back to face us. "All of them."

28

With a final smile, the Minister disappears again. The screen goes dark, back to being a window.

Suddenly space itself seems to shift in front of us. Where there should be nothing, where there *was* nothing, the blackness is shaking. And now dozens of ships appear out of nowhere, between us and where we need to go. Blocking our way out.

"Oh," is all Becka says, her voice unusually quiet.

The dark spots aren't easy to see against the blackness of space. But unlike before, when they were cloaked and completely invisible, we now know that they're here. The planet is protected by a blockade of ships, evenly spread out around Elvid IV like a net.

We're completely surrounded.

"They're everywhere," Ari says. "And we need to get *past* them to use the light speed engine."

It's hard to tell for sure, but it looks like all the ships are the same: small, speedy, triangular fighters. They're circling the planet in perfect formation, drawing criss-crossing lines with their exhaust smoke. The fighters are made of the same crystal as the buildings on Elvid IV: they're black and shiny and seem carved rather than constructed.

And each fighter has four large gunports—two on either side, facing front.

"Is this also part of the plan, Jack?" Principal Lochner says.

"No," I answer, staring into space. We can't use the light speed engine this close to the planet. And we can't go any farther ahead. "Shut the engines down."

It's over.

We've lost.

The ship jolts to a stop and we just drift—although maybe that's all we were ever doing.

"So that's it?" Ari asks.

I nod.

"No!" Becka insists. "That *can't* be it. Isn't there anything we can use to fight?"

"The ship doesn't have a firing system," Principal Lochner says, shaking its head.

Becka unbuckles her seatbelt and stands up. "What about the shuttles? Can we use the shuttles?"

"I don't think that evacuating this ship will do any good at this point," Principal Lochner says. "We'd still be trapped by that blockade."

"That's not what I mean!" Becka says impatiently.

Her eyes are darting back and forth as her mind works something out. "I heard you down in the hangar bay one time, mentioning a remote flight portal to Harriet. We don't have to use the shuttles to escape. We can use them to fight!"

Understanding dawns on Principal Lochner's face.

"You might be onto something," he says. "But we'll have to move quickly."

* * *

"*PROXIMITY ALERT,*" says the 118, tracking the progress of the tow ship. "*CONTACT IN THREE MINUTES.*"

We're in the cafeteria, and Principal Lochner is frantically pressing instructions into the main control panel. His fingers are swiping so fast across the screen that they're basically invisible. But he's still Principal Lochner: Even though pressing buttons isn't exactly extreme exercise, his forehead is covered in sweat and his cheeks are bright red. And for some reason, he's still wearing his suit jacket.

Becka runs in carrying four screens from the computer lab. "Got 'em," she reports.

"Good," Principal Lochner says without looking up.

She places the four screens down onto the only table left in the room. While she was gone, Ari and I shoved all the other tables, benches, and chairs into the kitchen.

We're going to need a clear view of every surface. The room needs to be completely empty—except for the one table and bench we pushed to the center, and the four screens Becka just put down.

"How do you know how to do all this stuff?" Ari asks Principal Lochner. I've got the same question. I had no idea that he was capable of doing *anything* except giving boring speeches and putting people in detention.

Principal Lochner smirks. "First," he explains, "I wasn't always a principal. I did a few years in the coast guard around Callisto. Picked up a thing or two. And second," he gently pats the wall nearest him like it's the fur of his childhood dog, "I've been on this ship for almost twenty years. I know it inside and out. It's a hunk of junk—"

"*THANKS.*"

"—but it's got some tricks left in it yet."

Tricks like the five shuttles in the hangar bay.

Rule Number One of computers is that if you have two of them—in any form—you can connect them to each other. You can link your ring to the 118's comm system. You can hook up your Pencil to the ice machine in the kitchen (which Ari did when we first left Elvid IV; he now gets crushed ice if he clicks five times and cubed if he clicks six times). And you can network a bunch of old shuttles into the ship's flight systems and operate them from inside the ship. Which was Becka's brilliant idea. It's possible that—between her secret parties, regular sneak-offs, and constant prank wars—she knows as much about the ship as Principal Lochner does.

The shuttles can't act as long-range drones or anything. We couldn't send them off to deep space. But as long as the 118 stays close enough to them to maintain an active signal, we can fly them from here. And with all their power diverted to the engines, they'll be speedy and hard to hit. We hope.

Five remote controlled shuttles. Our only protection. Our only weapons against a massive alien army. But we don't have to fight off the whole blockade. Only a few ships. We just need to poke a hole big enough to fly through, and then we're gone.

"There," Principal Lochner says, pressing down one last time on the room's main control panel.

"*SHUTTLE NETWORK INTERFACING COMPLETE*," the ship tells us. "*FLIGHT SYSTEMS ARE NOW INTEGRATED WITH REMOTE ACCESS TABLETS. NICE JOB, BY THE WAY.*"

"Ha!" Principal Lochner laughs. "A compliment from *you*? We really are in uncharted territory, aren't we?"

The moment we restart our engines—which will also be the moment those blockade ships come after us—Principal Lochner's going to open the hangar bay doors. Then, while we make a beeline for the blockade, we're going to remotely pilot the five shuttles as interference, as shields, maybe as giant missiles. Whatever it takes. All from this room.

"Ready?" Principal Lochner asks.

We just nod. We're about as ready as we're going to be.

Principal Lochner flips one more switch on the wall, activating the digital paper. See, just like on the *inside* of the ship, there are cameras all along the hull, facing out in every direction. But the bridge can't display everything going on outside the ship all at once. And according to Principal Lochner, if we're going to fend off an attack, we'll need to see everything, in 360 degrees.

"Cool," Becka says, as the cafeteria disappears.

It's like we're floating in space, with no PSS 118 around us. The planet is to our backs. Beneath our feet, above us, and in front of us are the stars and the moons and the ships blocking our way home. And far in the distance, we can see the suns at the center of this solar system. It's like we're inside a planetarium.

"This is awesome," Ari says.

"Except for that," I say, pointing to the long, black tow ship that's been speeding toward us from the surface of the planet.

"Right," Principal Lochner agrees. "And where's Harriet?"

Becka looks at me. "I thought you called her up here."

"I did," I answer. "She said she was coming."

"Harriet?" Principal Lochner speaks into the room's comm. "Your access to the ship has been restored, and we need you in the cafeteria immediately."

Static. And finally: "I'm so sorry," she says through the speaker. "I can't. I just can't."

"Harriet," Principal Lochner repeats. "We need your help."

Ari, Becka, and I look at each other nervously. Five shuttles equals five remote pilots. Me, Ari, Becka, Principal Lochner, Harriet.

"PROXIMITY ALERT: CONTACT IN TWO MINUTES."

"Please," she says. "You can handle it, right? I mean, those *kids*. They're incredible. Please don't make me."

Principal Lochner sighs and takes his hand off the comm button.

"I knew it was a bad idea to hire family," he says. "Harriet's actually my niece. She's a capable schoolship pilot. She can circle Ganymede over and over, slowly, and without any trouble—"

"AND EVEN THAT'S MOSTLY JUST ME," the ship interrupts.

"—but this is different," Principal Lochner says. He touches the screen again. "Okay, Harriet. We've got it here. Just keep everyone safe in the gym, okay?"

"Oh my gosh, thank you. Thank you, thank you."

Principal Lochner turns to us. "She's not totally off base, though, you know? You kids *have* been pretty incredible—"

We smile.

"—which is why I'm going to leave it to you here."

We stop smiling.

"What do you mean?" I ask him.

"I've decided to fly the ship from the bridge."

"But why?" Ari asks. "Can't you operate things from here? Isn't that the whole point?"

Principal Lochner nods. "This is the right place for you to fly the shuttles. But if we lose the networking feed, the 118's pilot needs to be up there. I'll be with you the whole time via the intercom. Don't worry."

"Principal Lochner?" I blurt out. I'm glad he's got faith in us. But I'm not stupid. We're just kids. "Shouldn't we see if Tim or Georgia will come up here and take Harriet's place? They've got to be more qualified than us, right?"

He gives us a face like—*Well* . . .—and asks, "Have you played Neptune Attacks?"

Not the response I was expecting.

Ari's eyes bug out of their sockets. He is more shocked that Principal Lochner has heard of our favorite video game than he was *when he found out that aliens are real.*

"Yeah," he whispers.

"Neptune Attacks 1 or 2?" I ask back.

Principal Lochner shrugs. "Doesn't matter," he answers. "But I like one better than two."

"Ha!" Ari shouts at me.

Principal Lochner turns to Becka, who says: "Of course I've played them. And you and Ari are right. One is so much better than two."

I look over at Ari, who is staring at Becka. And maybe it's because Becka already knows about Ari's crush. Maybe it's because we're about to fly headfirst into a space battle. Or maybe it's because, after you've escaped from jail and gone back in time and flown a spaceship, everything else is a breeze. So Ari stutters: "Would you, would you want to play multiplayer some time?"

And Becka doesn't hesitate. "Sure!"

Principal Lochner clears his throat. "Good." He heads toward the doors. "Then you're all just as qualified as the crew. This is going to be a lot more like those games than what the 118 experiences day-to-day. Now divide the shuttles among yourselves and wait for my signal. Good luck."

And with that, our middle-school principal leaves us alone to take control of the only things that can protect us from a giant alien army, the only things giving us any hope of getting home alive.

You know, usual summer vacation stuff.

29

"PROXIMITY ALERT," the ship warns. *"CONTACT IN ONE MINUTE."*

We're sitting at the table in the middle of the cafeteria. Ari is in the center and Becka and I are sitting on either side of him. We're facing forward, staring at the approaching tow ship and the blockade separating us from freedom.

Becka turns to me. "How many do you want?"

With Principal Lochner flying the 118, we need to split up responsibility for remotely flying the shuttles. Two, two, and one.

"Why don't you each take two?" I say.

Becka's eyes light up. "Are you sure?" she asks.

"Positive," I say, meaning it. I have a feeling that she's going to be pretty good at this. Probably better than me. And Ari controlling two is a no-brainer: he's been training for a moment like this his whole life. So I call up controls for one of the five shuttles and Becka and Ari do the same for the other four.

"You okay?" I ask Ari.

He shakes his head and looks over at me. "I'm sorry about the mutiny," he tells me. "You're my best friend. And I never—"

"I know," I interrupt. "I'm sorry too. And it'll be fine. We'll be fine. We'll make it."

"And, um," he says, squirming to face Becka. But he draws a blank and trails off.

She smiles at him. It's almost—and please don't quote me on this—sweet. "We can do this," Becka declares.

"Yeah," he says back, his voice calm. "Okay."

"*PROXIMITY ALERT,*" the ship says again. "*CONTACT IN FIFTEEN SECONDS. IT'S NOW OR NEVER.*"

"This is it," Principal Lochner's voice booms over the loudspeaker. "I'm going to take the 118 straight out, away from the planet. As soon as we're beyond the jamming—the *moment* you can, Jack—use the light speed engine to get us out of here."

"Got it," I say.

Principal Lochner restarts the engines with a rumble. "See you on the other side."

The 118 lurches forward, squeaking past the tow ship just before its jaws close around the hull.

At the same time, a few of the blockade ships break off from their revolutions around the planet. They're coming to intercept us. Three of them—no, four. Four of the arrowhead-shaped fighters are heading straight for us.

"Opening the aft doors," Principal Lochner announces. "Take 'em out."

The 118 shivers as the two large hangar doors open up at the back of the ship. For now, the fighters heading our way think they outnumber us four to one. But they're about to be surprised. As soon as the shuttles are out there, it'll be five—six, if you include the 118 itself—against four. Although, considering that it's also four ships *with* guns versus six ships with no guns, it doesn't exactly even the odds.

I use my screen to move one of the shuttles out of the hangar bay, positioning it at the very front of the ship.

Becka moves her two shuttles in formation with mine, putting one directly above the ship and the other below, while Ari places his on either side, surrounding the 118.

"Uh oh," Ari says. Two more Elvidian ships have broken off from the blockade and are heading straight toward us. Six against six. Great.

"I see them," I say.

"Hold tight," Principal Lochner says, tilting the 118 to the side in some sad attempt at a zigzag evasive maneuver. He's actually a decent pilot—but the schoolship wasn't built for a dogfight. "Don't be afraid to lose the shuttles. Do what you have to."

The gun turrets on the enemy ships shine purple and electric, like pent-up balls of lightning about to unravel. The lights give the hulls of the black ships an eerie glow, which makes them even scarier. Their hulls are flawlessly sleek. No doors. No windows. Aside from the guns, the ships don't look like they have any parts at all. Part of me suspects—hopes, maybe—that they're unpiloted drones.

"One is firing!" Ari says, reading a display on his screen.

We watch helplessly as the leader of the four fighters gets a shot off. I consider trying to fly my own shuttle into its path. But it's too late. Lightning crackles toward us, nothing like a laser. It's both more natural and more unnatural at the same time.

"Hold on!" Principal Lochner shouts.

But miraculously, we barely feel it.

"Damage report?" I ask.

Ari checks. "We're okay," he says, relieved.

"*SPEAK FOR YOURSELF*," the ship adds.

"But it only grazed us," Ari explains. "Scorched the upper hull. No breaches."

"Ha," Becka says, laughing. "Bad shots, huh?"

"No, they're testing us," Principal Lochner says. "They want to see if we're going to fire back. What our capabilities are."

The ships are getting closer, weapons still charged and locked on. In a few seconds, the other two will catch up and we'll be in even worse trouble than we are now.

Time to punch a hole in this blockade.

I crank up my shuttle's engines to full speed and aim it straight for the group of four fighters. I flash its front lights, hoping that they make it seem like our (unarmed) shuttle is charging up to fire its (nonexistent) weapons.

They're expecting me to shoot at them. They're not expecting me to *ram* them. So I get pretty close before one of the Elvidian fighters fires directly at the shuttle, striking its engines and throwing it off balance. I try to regain control and make its path too erratic to follow. The shuttle is moving fast. But another ship fires at it and that second lightning strike hits it in the nose and splits it in two, like a knife slicing through bread.

On the bright side, I still caught them off guard. I was moving the small ship so fast that, when it finally comes apart, one of the halves breaks off and hurtles back toward the fighters.

It connects with one of the Elvidian ships, which gets knocked off its own course, spins wildly, and passes directly in front of a second fighter that's just now shooting off another lightning bolt. That bolt hits the out-of-control fighter head on, at close range. It explodes into a ball of fire and goes hurtling toward the surface of Elvid IV.

The other three fighters scatter in the chaos as Becka pushes another remote controlled shuttle forward. One of the Elvidian ships does a last-minute barrel roll away from the wreckage of the destroyed fighter—and Becka moves her shuttle into its path, forcing a direct collision.

"That's two down!" I yell, pumped up on my own adrenaline.

"Yeah!" Becka shouts. She's sacrificed one of her shuttles too, but we're making progress.

"Take my other shuttle," Ari tells me, transferring control of one of the two he's operating.

"Thanks!"

"*ALMOST THERE,*" the ship says. "*THIRTY SECONDS UNTIL WE'RE BEYOND THE JAMMING.*"

My heart is pounding. I'm not sure we *have* thirty seconds. The two fighters that were farther out have closed in and joined a loose formation with the other two, surrounding us on all sides. We're again facing four Elvidian ships. But we only have three shuttles left. And while our attackers are all close to *us*, they're staying far enough away from each other to make themselves less vulnerable to debris.

"I'm sending one in," Ari says. "I'll—"

Before he can do anything, the ships around us open fire simultaneously.

In an instant, Ari's and Becka's shuttles both explode. I try to move the last of the small ships—the one Ari gave over to my control—to the front, where we need the most protection. *We're almost there. Come on. Come on.* But the Elvidian ships open fire again, blowing the little shuttle into a thousand shards of metal. The 118 shudders and groans as it's hit by the pieces. The room rocks to one side. And the table we're sitting at slides across the room and into the wall. We manage to stumble off of the attached bench before it drags us down along with it. But it hits the digital paper so hard that the wall cracks from the floor to the ceiling and the display disappears, leaving us with a huge blind spot to our left.

"*LIFE SUPPORT AT 74 PERCENT!*" the ship informs us. "*HULL BREACH IN LOWER CREW QUARTERS!*"

"That sounds bad," Becka says, staring out at the blockade of ships.

"*YOU THINK?*" screeches the ship. "*LIFE SUPPORT AT 68 PERCENT! YOU'LL BE OUT OF OXYGEN IN MINUTES!*"

That last blast threw us off course and we're now drifting sideways, instead of straight away from the planet. Principal Lochner has lost control. But worse, we're no longer being hunted by only four ships. The entire blockade is moving toward us now.

"Principal Lochner?!" I yell, hoping that he can still hear me from the bridge. I try to push down the nausea that's overwhelming my brain. The room shakes and the remaining digital paper panels show our surroundings going around and around.

He doesn't answer.

"Ari?" I ask. "I don't think Principal Lochner's piloting us anymore. Can you control the ship from here?"

"I don't know!" he screams.

We're yelling at the top our lungs, both because of the rising panic inside our heads and because the ship is blaring out warnings—proximity, targeting, damage.

Ahead of us—no, now that we're spinning out of control, *behind* us—one of the fighters fires again. All the wallpaper goes black, plunging the room into familiar darkness that's only broken up by the blinking red emergency lights running along the edges of the ceiling. The ship banks hard to one side and Ari jumps up to his feet.

"I've lost the networking feed!" he screams, terrified. "We need to get back to the bridge! I can't control anything from here!"

We're hit again. And hit again. I don't know how the ship is holding together. I guess the 118 is stronger than the shuttles. But it's still creaking and groaning, threatening to come apart at the seams. The alarms are shrieking and the ship is screaming out its unhelpful warnings: *"AHHH! SECONDARY FUSION REACTOR CRITICAL! HULL BREACH IN LOWER CREW QUARTERS! LIFE SUPPORT AT 62 PERCENT!"*

"Shut up!" I yell.

"I CAN'T! IT'S PART OF MY PROGRAM-MING—HULL BREACH IN FACULTY OFFICES. LIFE SUPPORT AT 57 PERCENT!"

We run—stumble—out of the cafeteria and down the hall back toward the bridge. We can feel the ship straining to keep itself together. *"HULL BREACH IN SCIENCE LAB 2! LIFE SUPPORT AT 56 PERCENT!"*

As we sprint down the corridor, sparks fly out from a nearby computer console. One of them hits the sleeve of Becka's T-shirt, which catches fire.

"I'm fine!" she yells, slapping her shoulder to put out the flame. "I'm fine! Keep going!"

"I WAS WRONG ABOUT HAVING MINUTES! OXYGEN DEPLETION IMMINENT!"

The doors to the bridge are stuck shut. The controls don't work, so I have to kick-smash the glass in a small manual override underneath the computer access panel and crank one door open by hand. We squeeze painfully sideways to enter the room.

"LIFE SUPPORT AT 51 PERCENT! OH NO, OH NO. NOT THE—FUEL LEAK IN PROGRESS! FUEL LEAK IN PROGRESS!"

It's a disaster in here. The main front window looks dangerously cracked. One more direct hit and it'll prob-ably shatter, sucking us out into open space. Ari's old computer station is on fire, crackling as the flames reach up to the charred roof. A broken sprinkler system spits out a little water that evaporates before it even hits the ground.

There's a fire extinguisher attached to the back wall by the door. Becka grabs it and puts out the flames before they spread to the thick carpet and blaze out of control.

Principal Lochner is slumped over in the captain's chair, buckled tight into the seat. I grab hold of his arm and feel for a pulse. He's alive. Passed out—with a bruise on his head where he must've been hit by something—but alive.

And even though he's unconscious, his fingers are gripped tight around Doctor's Shrew's cage, which he must have picked up and kept safe. Doctor Shrew looks fine. He's still going to town on that one stalk of celery I gave him, totally oblivious.

I tuck the cage underneath Becka's computer station, hoping he won't rattle around too badly down there.

Ari runs over to Becka's station too. He touches it. And nothing happens. I'm scared that we've lost total control up here too. That there's nothing we can do.

"Ahhh!" Ari screams. He clenches his fists and brings them down hard onto the computer screen in frustration—bringing the console back to life.

"*WEL—ZONA—MAN.*"

Barely.

We sit down and strap in—Ari and I by Becka's computer station, and Becka by Ari's old and busted console. We see one of the fighters zip past us, firing at the hull as it flies by.

"Are we almost in the clear?!" Becka screams.

"I have no idea!" Ari replies. "The ship's lost its navigation scanner!"

The ship is still spinning in the right direction, away from the planet—but in the chaos, we've lost ground. We're surrounded on all sides and these fighters seem bent on blowing us up right here and now. "Ship?" I ask. "Are we out of range of the light speed jamming?"

"*NEGATIVE! LOW ORBIT LIGHT SPEED INTERFERENCE REMAINS—*"

We're out of time. The rest of the ships are almost on top of us. Their weapons light up, a thousand electric purple lights on a thousand open gunports, all aimed at our little schoolship.

"Can this thing still fly?" I ask.

"Not for long," he says, pulling back on a lever. "But I'll get us as far as I can."

We keep speeding away from the planet. But it's just not fast enough.

"Ship," I ask again. "Can we use the light speed engine?"

"*NO! LOW ORB—SPEE—RENCE—*"

The 118 is dying.

"Ship!" I shout desperately, one last time, just as the Elvidians open fire. "Can we use the light speed engine now?"

I hold my breath. Everything's hanging in the balance. All I can think about is my dad and how—even if you mean well, even if you try to do the right thing—you never know where your choices are going to lead.

"*AFF—*"

Good enough for me.

"Light speed engine, now, destination, Earth," I say, looking over at Ari and Becka. "Engage."

30

I sense it more than I see it or hear it. It's not an explosion. Just a coming apart. Like the individual atoms inside my body are fighting against whatever keeps them together. Remember that first time we used the light speed engine? When I said that it felt like life went dark? Well, this feels the same. Only then, the darkness lasted for a moment. This time, it's longer. Everything's just . . . blank. I'm losing myself. Slipping away into pieces. I know that I'm supposed to come back together. Reappear. But I can't. Maybe I shouldn't. How did I get here? Do I know who I am? Where—

Boom.

My eyes snap open. I'm crumpled over in the chair behind one of the computer consoles, still regaining feeling in my arms and legs. The light on the bridge is bright—too bright for me to see anything but colors and shapes. All I make out through the window is what looks like the remnants of a fiery shockwave spreading out from around the ship. I'm still lightheaded and can't think clearly. Did we make it to Earth?

Somebody's screaming.

"Jack!"

My vision clears and, fighting the pain, I turn my neck to the side. Ari, Becka, and Principal Lochner. Right where I left them. An alarm is shrieking in the background.

Ari is staring helplessly down at the smoking computer terminal in front of us and Becka, like me, is only now regaining consciousness. Principal Lochner is still passed out in the captain's chair. And the ship is in the worst shape of all.

I can feel it in the chair, in the floor, and in the walls. The ship is coming apart.

The engines are useless. Most of the power is gone. And we're plummeting straight down, shooting through cloud after cloud as we get lower. I'm trying to see something—anything—out the front window. But it's still only blue and white for now.

Blue and white.

The sky. This is the *sky*. And not just any sky. This is *Earth's* sky. I'd recognize it anywhere. From books, TV, magazines, holofilms. If you don't know what the sky looks like, you're not really human.

It worked.

We bank hard to one side as an air current overpowers our lifeless ship.

It sort of worked.

I mean, our ship is toast. But we came out of light speed, alive. We didn't explode or implode or dissolve or whatever else might happen when you go to light speed in a ship that's been beaten to a pulp.

The ship spins around again. And, as Ari fights to regain control, he pulls too strongly to one side and we flip over two, no three, times.

We're here. But we're crashing.

"Can't you do anything?" Becka groans from her chair. She's buckled in, holding on to her computer station for dear life.

Ari presses a few buttons and pulls a few levers, but nothing slows us down. As we enter the lower atmosphere, through the front window, I can see the telltale fire of reentry burning too hot.

Suddenly Ari jolts upright and turns some switch from underneath his station.

"There!" he shouts, and the ship jerks backward, moaning in pain.

But after a few seconds, we settle out a little. We feel steadier.

"What did you do?" I scream over the noise.

"I opened the hangar!" he answers.

Ari pulls down on one of the two hangar door releases with every ounce of his strength—he even needs to prop his legs up against a nearby panel to get enough force behind his grip—and the ship banks hard to the left. He lets go. The ship rights itself. He pulls the other one. And we tilt to the right with a jerky, dizzying jolt.

"You can control it?!" Becka yells.

"Yeah!" Ari answers. "There are two huge doors back there! I switched the controls to manual. We can use them like sails, see?"

"Ari!" Becka shouts with approval. "You're a genius!"

True. But I'm not sure it's enough this time.

The ship spins in a full circle as Ari loses his grip on one of the reins and leans exhaustedly against the other like he's about to collapse. I try to help him control the hangar bay levers, but we're still not slowing down enough. Gravity is gravity. The engines are completely dead and if we hit the ground at this speed it won't matter if we can turn a bit to the right or left, or if we splat against the surface at a few hundred miles per hour less.

"Where we are we?" I shout to Becka.

"External sensors are down!" she screams.

The clouds part and it's now terrifyingly clear that we're not as high up as I thought we were. In the distance—but not far enough away by a long shot—I spot a familiar shoreline. Massive city walls protect impossibly tall skyscrapers from the surrounding water. And of course I recognize the small green statue near the bottom edge of the island.

I grip the sides of my chair even more tightly. On any other day, I'd be thrilled to be here. It would be a dream come true. But not today. Because there probably isn't any *worse* place to crash land a spaceship than into the middle of New York City.

"Turn down! Head for the river!" I shout.

"I'm trying!"

Our best bet would be to fall straight into the water. But we're not coming in steep enough. Most of the ocean is already behind us and even the rigged hangar doors can't send us into a nosedive.

Out toward the left side of the bridge window, we see boathouses and stores and apartment buildings and a large grassy lawn. Over on the right and up ahead, countless towers gleam in the sunlight, stretching north for miles. We can't go too far to either side. And the ship won't let us go straight down.

We're close enough now that I can make out George Washington Bridge Park directly ahead. Ari and I did an Earth Fair project on it once. It connects New York to New Jersey across a river and hasn't been used for old wheelcars since, well, whenever we stopped using old wheelcars. These days, it's a park. A *popular* park. The sun is beaming. There's barely a cloud in the sky. It's the kind of summer day that would draw people out.

But the closer grassy space on our left looks empty. Big and empty.

"I'm gonna aim for that park!" Ari shouts, pointing ahead and to our left.

"It's just like a runway!" I tell him. If we had full

control over the ship, there'd be plenty of room to take the 118 down safely. But we don't have full control over the ship.

We've got only one chance to save ourselves without doing damage to the city. At this rate, we'll never land safely in the grass. We're too low down already. We need to skid directly onto the water and hope we come to a soft enough landing by the time we hit the empty shore.

"Right!" I scream. "Right!"

We jerk to the side, barely avoiding clipping the edges of a giant building.

"Too much! Left! Left!"

We readjust at the last second. But even though the river is wide, we're moving fast. We dip and smack hard against the New Jersey side, too early. A giant chunk of the seawall breaks off, nearly crushing a building beneath it. We get turned around and spin back out the way we came.

"Steady!" I yell.

Through the window, I can see pieces of our ship that have come off in the descent. Fiery metal is flying everywhere. I hope there aren't any boats underneath us and that everyone else is okay down in the gym.

The 118 shudders as another piece of the hull goes flying by, knocked loose. Flat and sharp, it lodges itself into the cliff now on our right.

One of the hangar doors.

"Hold on!" Ari shouts.

The ship turns around and around, unbalanced and completely out of control.

We're screaming at the top of our lungs. Everything is moving so quickly now. And I only know we've touched down when we smack the water and I'm almost thrown out of my chair. Huge waves spout up on all sides of us and the room begins filling with water, which seeps through the walls. But the ship doesn't come to a stop. Instead it *bounces*, like a pebble skipped across a lake, and rises back up into the air.

I can feel everything I've ever eaten in my stomach, churning like I'm on a rollercoaster. We clear the park Ari was aiming for—blocks of other buildings pass directly beneath us—and finally slam down hard into *another* river, flowing just behind the first one. We're far enough away from New York City now that we don't have to worry about it. But there's another city directly ahead of us.

As we hit the water again, the front window shatters, spraying glass and salt water into the bridge. I duck, covering my face with my arms.

We skid forward, this time sliding along the water like it's a solid sheet of ice. We're careening to the side, directly toward the city. We jump the riverbank and run aground on a wide street surrounded by towers of metal and glass. We're flailing down an avenue, inches away from the buildings around us. I hear a loud scratching sound as the ship tears up the street in its wake.

Until little by little, we slow down.

And stop.

Alive.

I can't believe it. We're alive. On Earth. We made it. I turn my head around to look at Ari and Becka. They're as shocked as I am. Principal Lochner is just starting to regain consciousness. He's going to be sorry he missed this (or, then again, maybe not). And one glance at Doctor Shrew confirms that he's still having a perfectly normal day. He glances up at me for maybe half a second before he goes back to snacking.

Looking at Doctor Shew, I can't help it—I start laughing. And not a normal laugh either. A full, whole-body-shaking laugh. I'm cracking up and Ari and Becka do the same. I know that there's still a lot to worry about. We just crash landed into a pretty big city near New York. I'm scared that we may have hurt people. And there's still the big question of what the Quarantine did to the people on Ganymede and whether the Minister is sending someone after us. But for the moment, none of that matters: I'm alive and I'm cracking up.

The ship flickers back to life just long enough to say: *"SO PRETTY MUCH AN AVERAGE 118 LAND-ING, EH?"* Which isn't really that funny. But this is one of those moments where *everything* is funny.

After a minute I calm down—and look out of the huge hole in front of me, where the bridge's main window used to be. I expect to see crowds of people or firefighters starting to gather. But there's no one. I'm relieved. Maybe there was some kind of surface proximity alarm that got everyone to safety.

"Come on!" I say, standing up. I'm bruised and my legs and arms feel like jelly. But otherwise, I'm all right. "Let's get out of here!"

We *could* use the door and wind through the ship toward the main exit. But why bother when there's a new opening right in front of us.

"Let's just hop out the window," I suggest.

"Awesome," Ari agrees.

"Um . . . wait," Becka says.

"Wait?" I ask. "For what?"

I look back at Ari and Becka, who are now both huddled around Becka's console. I guess it's back up and running, although I don't know what they're looking at. We don't need a damage report to tell us that the ship is busted.

But fine, if they want to stay here and look at screens all day, that's up to them. So I step over the edge of the window and onto the nose of the ship. The 118 juts out about twenty feet from the front of the bridge. I test the stability of the hull with one foot before stepping outside with all my weight. For the first time in my life, I feel the warmth of the sun. The *real* sun. When I'm done with school, I'm *totally* moving to Earth.

"Come on!" I call over my shoulder. "You have to come out here."

I take another step forward, crunching a pile of broken glass underneath my feet. It's so quiet that I can hear every little thing. The ship settling. A nearby fire crackling. And Ari and Becka slowly walking across the bridge and up toward me. I hear more footsteps. Principal Lochner stumbles off the bridge, holding his head. And behind him, the rest of the 118ers pile out too, taking stunned steps out into the sun.

We all stare at what's ahead of us. The street is completely *empty*. We're in the middle of a large intersection, hovercars sprinkled down each of the roads. At first, I thought that *we* had knocked them down. But now I see that they're not just bunched up around where the 118 crashed. They're everywhere. Piled on the ground. Jammed into the sides of nearby buildings.

It's as if, all at once, every single hovercar fell out of the sky.

I look up. There are flames in the distance all across this city. I look behind me, across the little river, and see more plumes of smoke dotting the horizon. But not a single siren.

And no people anywhere. No stranded hovercar drivers, no gawkers watching us from the windows of buildings, no panicked pedestrians. Even if there was a surface proximity alarm, *someone* would still be outside.

"Where are all the people?" I wonder out loud. But even as I'm saying it, Bale Kontra's explanation of the

Quarantine comes rushing back to me. And I realize that I misunderstood. The Quarantine *was* bigger than the 118. Much bigger.

"That's what I was trying to tell you," Becka says. "The ship didn't pick up any human life signs." She pauses, lowering her voice to almost a whisper. *"Anywhere."*

31

Principal Lochner smiles and adjusts his tie—the same one that he wore on the last day of school.

"Where were we?" he jokes. "I think we had just finished the slideshow."

You can feel the whole school roll its eyes so hard that the ship might flip over.

"Anyway," he continues, "I know we've all been through a lot. And the last thing you probably want is an assembly."

Actually, I don't mind. We've been waiting two whole days for the teachers to talk to us about what we're going to do next, and I'm more than ready for an update. Though I do mind that we're sitting in the cafeteria of our mostly-destroyed schoolship when we could be having this meeting ANYWHERE ON THE ENTIRE PLANET. We could at least take a field trip ten minutes away to New York City, right? Empire State Building. Coney Island. Do you know how badly I want to go to the beach?

Instead the teachers put out the usual folding chairs and are having us sit by grade in our broken-down ship, still hammered into the streets of Newark, New Jersey, where we crashed. I'm in the front row with Becka and Ari. Becka never would've sat with us before all this happened, but now it feels totally natural.

"We've given you some time to rest up and absorb our . . . situation," Principal Lochner says. "But all of us—we're important. Too important to sit on our hands any longer."

Out of nowhere, one of the last remaining roof tiles falls and hits the floor a foot away from him.

"So where is everyone?" one of the fifth graders yells from the back. Antonio, I think.

"We don't know," Principal Lochner answers honestly. "And please raise your hand if you have a question."

"Seriously?" Antonio snaps back.

Principal Lochner gives his classic eyebrow raise and I turn around to glance at Antonio. He grunts and raises his hand.

"Yes, Antonio?" Principal Lochner calls.

"Um, seriously?" he asks again.

"Thank you," Lochner says firmly. "And yes, seriously. Just because we've hit some . . . bumps in the road doesn't mean that we can't stay civilized. And as I was saying, we've rested long enough. It's time for a plan."

I look sideways at Ari and Becka. We're back to being plain old kids, just along for the ride. It's a serious relief. Once we explained everything, Principal Lochner decided not to punish us for all the trouble we caused. "You three have managed to do things that I don't think most adults could have done," he told us yesterday. "And you showed bravery in the face of real danger, when some of us would have given up." He paused. "When some of us *did* give up."

After all the times I was sent to the principal's office this year, it felt weird to sit across from him and get *complimented*. But I guess the mistakes the Grahams have made don't have to be the full story here. Technically, we did save the 118 from the Quarantine, even if we messed up a lot along the way.

And our classmates don't seem to hate us either. If anything, we've gained popularity points. Even me.

In fact, just before the assembly, Riya Windsor came over to me to say that she was sorry about my dad. That she knew the last few months had been hard for me and that it hadn't really been fair. Which was pretty cool.

"So here's the situation," Principal Lochner explains "They're out there, somewhere. Likely teleported far away by an Elvidian process called the Quarantine. And as the only ones who are still free, we have a responsibility to search for our friends and families and the whole human race. It's our job to bring them home."

The teachers and crew are standing in a line next to Principal Lochner. Most of them—except the ever-unimpressed Mrs. Watts—are nodding like they're listening to the president give some important speech. And I have to admit, Principal Lochner's really stepped up to the plate. The teachers aren't the ideal rescue party for the entire human race. But if three kids and a hamster can pull off what we did, there's no telling what the whole school—together—is capable of.

"To do that," he continues, "we need a ship. We need this ship."

Half the room groans.

"*DON'T ALL CHEER AT ONCE,*" the ship says. The AI's fully back online, even if most of the rest of it isn't.

Most of our classmates were hoping that we'd ditch the 118 and find some other ship to fly, like a military carrier or maybe a luxury cruise liner. Something with a waterslide.

But I knew that Principal Lochner would make this choice.

"The 118 is the only ship we have that can travel faster than light. Which means that, step one, we need to repair it. When the assembly is over, you'll all get your work assignments. Small groups of students will be paired with a teacher and given a system to work on. Life support. Hull integrity. School components. Engineeri—"

"Wait." Antonio again.

Principal Lochner puts his hands on his waist. "Yes?" he asks, after Antonio remembers to raise his hand.

"School components? Like . . . the classrooms and stuff?"

"Exactly."

"But what for? Don't we have better things to do?"

"We have a crucial mission. True. But that doesn't diminish the importance of your education. In fact, it makes it even more important. It's summer right now, so we'll give you a break. But if our search takes a long time—and it might—school will start in the fall like it always does. The fifth graders will start sixth grade, the sixth graders will start seventh, and the seventh graders—even though the 118 technically only goes up through seventh—they'll start eighth. In fact, Mr. Cardegna is already hard at work planning the curriculum for eighth grade English Lit."

"Summer reading lists by the end of the week!" Mr. Cardegna announces.

More groans. But I don't know—I wouldn't mind a little "normal" in my life.

"We'll figure out the details as we go along," Principal Lochner tells us. "But I also wanted to say that you've all been incredible. I couldn't be prouder. We've got the best school in the solar system. And when we bring everyone back—not if, but *when*—they're going know it too."

"St. Andrew's Prep sucks!" Ming yells from the row behind me.

Everyone starts laughing and wooing. Even Principal Lochner lets out a chuckle.

"Settle down, settle down." He waits a beat. "But go Champions!"

And it's weird, considering how much has gone wrong, but that gets the room cheering louder than we've ever cheered for ourselves before.

I feel Ari take a deep breath and exhale. I look over at him. Things are good with us now. I'm really going to try to be a better friend. Hopefully, it doesn't take a *second* unimaginable alien conspiracy to keep me focused on what's really important.

Principal Lochner raises his hands up in the air to quiet us down again.

"Seriously, though," he says. "This isn't going to be easy. But I *know* we can do this. We can bring everyone home. We can save the world."

"No we can't!" someone shouts. Hunter LaFleur. Obviously. "We're just a bunch of kids. You're only teachers. This is a *school*. How can we possibly save the world?"

The room goes suddenly silent again, like we're all holding our breath. But Principal Lochner is undeterred. "Aliens or no aliens, there's no such thing as *just* kids. No such thing as *only* teachers. Schools are where we make the future. There's nothing we can't accomplish. So I have to ask, are you with me?"

He lets the question hang out there, dangling over us. It's a little awkward and a little forced—and, at first, it goes unanswered.

"I'm gonna ask again," he says louder, like he's trying to get us excited for a homecoming game. "Are. You. With. Me?"

"Yeah!" Becka shouts. Ari and I echo her. We owe Principal Lochner that much, at least.

"Are you with me?"

"*FINE*," the ship mutters. But more kids join in now. The teachers too: "Yeah!"

"Are you with me?"

"Yeah!"

The room shakes and he nods, grinning from ear to ear. And maybe he's right. Maybe we really can do this. Bring everyone home. Save the world.

"Okay," he says. "Then let's get started."

ACKNOWLEDGMENTS

I wrote my first book when I was in fifth grade. It was a novelization of the Super Nintendo game *The Death and Return of Superman*. It was handwritten on wide-ruled, loose-leaf paper. And it was EVERYTHING to me. Until I mustered up the courage to share it with one of the bigger kids on the school bus, who made me painfully aware that *The Death and Return of Superman* was already a book of sorts and that the SNES game had been based on an acclaimed comic book series (which itself had already spawned a novelization). Having legitimately thought that I'd penned The Definitive Retelling of My Second-Favorite Video Game (I wasn't worthy of *The Legend of Zelda: A Link to the Past*), I regrettably chucked my version in the trash.

Since then, I've mostly kept wanting to write fiction to myself. All this is a self-indulgent windup to deeply thanking the small handful of friends who did know and who have encouraged me all this while. Thank you.

I'm throwing out a trite "you know who you are"—because you do. And because if you *didn't* know this was something I've been chasing, it's not you, it's me. I promise to shout more from rooftops (or flight decks) from now on.

To my will-not-be-deterred agent, Elana Roth Parker, thank you so very much for seeing something in this book and sticking with it, even though it took more than a few light-years.

Thank you to Lerner/Carolrhoda, especially my editor, Amy Fitzgerald. Thank you for taking a chance on the PSS 118, and for helping me polish the hull until it shined. (Well, okay, not *shined*. It *is* the PSS 118, after all.)

Serena. This is as good a place as any to thank you for being kind and curious in your unique and extraordinary way. I love you to the moon (to the very last moon).

And Tali. No one's read this thing more than you have. No one's encouraged me more than you have. No one has as seriously, as confidently, and as unsarcastically known all along that I'd eventually be able to thank you in these pages one day. You're always eyeing some star beyond your reach and I hope Serena learns a thing or two from you about the power of well-placed wanderlust. I know I have.

ABOUT THE AUTHOR

Joshua S. Levy was born and raised in Florida. After teaching middle school (yes, including seventh grade) for a little while, he went to law school. He lives with his wife and daughter in New Jersey, where he practices as a lawyer. Unfortunately, outer space doesn't come up in court nearly as often as he'd like. *Seventh Grade vs. the Galaxy* is his first novel. You can find him online at www.joshuasimonlevy.com and on Twitter @JoshuaSLevy.